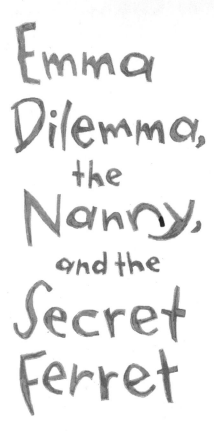

Emma Dilemma, the Nanny, and the Secret Ferret

by Patricia Hermes

Marshall Cavendish Children

For Madeline Victoria Hermes,
my very own Emma

Marshall Cavendish Corporation
99 White Plains Road
Tarrytown, NY 10591
www.marshallcavendish.us/kids

Library of Congress Cataloging-in-Publication Data
Hermes, Patricia.
Emma dilemma, the nanny, and the secret ferret / by Patricia Hermes. — 1st ed.
p. cm.
Summary: Emma struggles with finding the perfect time to confess to her
parents that she brought her pet ferret on vacation to Maine, and trying to
save her favorite tree that a new neighbor wants to cut down.
ISBN 978-0-7614-5650-6
[1. Vacations—Fiction. 2. Trees—Fiction. 3. Ferrets as pets—Fiction.
4. Family life—Maine—Fiction. 5. Maine—Fiction.] I. Title.
PZ7.H4317Emv 2010
[Fic]--dc22
2009039579

Book design by Virginia Pope
Editor: Margery Cuyler

Printed in China (E)
First edition
10 9 8 7 6 5 4 3 2 1

mc Marshall Cavendish
Children

Other **Emma Dilemma** Books

Emma Dilemma and the New Nanny
Emma Dilemma and the Two Nannies
Emma Dilemma and the Soccer Nanny
Emma Dilemma and the Camping Nanny

McClain

Dad

Emma

Annie

Lizzie + Ira

Tim

Mom

Contents

Chapter One

Packing for Vacation

Emma's room was a mess. A big, fat mess. A worse-than-usual, big, fat mess.

"A charming room with personality," Annie, Emma's beloved nanny, always said.

"A jungle," Mom sometimes said.

Emma blew her bangs out of her eyes and plopped down onto the window seat. She looked around. Mom was more right than Annie this time—Emma's room was a jungle. Jeans, shirts, shorts, bathing suits, sweatshirts, and undies were tumbled all over the bed. Woof, the family's huge poodle, was sprawled out asleep on top of everything. The books that Emma had been packing were toppled into a lopsided heap on the floor.

Marshmallow, one of Emma's pet ferrets, had climbed to the top of her bookshelf and was surveying the mess from where she was perched. Marmaduke, Emma's other ferret, was hungrily sniffing at her backpack, looking for any sticky, leftover candy. There was usually plenty of that, dried up and stuck to the bottom. Emma's heart did a sad, tiny thump when she thought about spending all summer without her ferrets, ferrets whom she loved more than just about anything in the world.

She bent over and gently scooped Marmaduke into her lap. His little nose twitched, and his shiny black eyes looked up at her sweetly. She lifted him to her shoulder so he could look around, then leaned back in the window seat. She'd been packing all morning, and she needed a break.

The whole family was packing—Mom; Daddy; Emma's big brother Tim; the little kids, McClain and Ira and Lizzie. And Annie, the best nanny in the whole, wide world, was helping everyone. Tomorrow they were leaving for their summer house in Maine.

Emma loved the house in Maine. It was so different from home, where she had to check in with the grown-ups before she did a single solitary thing or went anywhere, even to the park or a friend's house.

In Maine, she played in the woods with other

kids, or often just by herself. She had a favorite tree that towered over the deer path. She spent hours in that tree, reading or watching deer walk quietly down the path right beneath her. Some days, she scattered apples on the ground for the deer. From her seat high in the tree, she could see, and even hear, the deer munching away. At night sometimes, the whole family lay on the dock together, looking up at the sky and watching for star showers. If it wasn't too cold, the family even swam together in the dark. Emma was a great swimmer and loved the water.

And there was an extra good thing about Maine—Max, Emma's cousin. He and his parents, Uncle Max and Auntie Liz, Mom's twin sister, also had a summer house on the lake, just a few houses away from their own. Max was exactly Emma's age, and he liked exactly the same things she did. Sometimes Mom and Daddy called him Horrible Max, but not in a mean way. It was just because Max often got into trouble—with Emma.

Just thinking of the trees and the lake, the deer, and the awesome quiet at night made Emma almost shiver with happiness. She lifted her head and smiled, imagining that she could even smell the pine trees.

Tomorrow. Tomorrow, she'd be there.

The only bad thing was leaving Marshmallow and Marmaduke. Last year, both ferrets had caused all sorts of trouble at the lake house. Marmaduke had gotten stuck in the fold-up couch, and Daddy had had to unscrew all the hinges in order to get him out without hurting him. While they had been doing that, Marshmallow had chewed through the hose of the washing machine, spraying water all over the place. And lots of other really bad stuff. This year, Mom had laid down the law: no ferrets in Maine.

Luisa, one of Emma's best friends, had agreed to care for Marshmallow. Luisa just loved her. Whenever Luisa came over to Emma's house, Marshmallow crawled up inside Luisa's shirt. That meant that Marshmallow felt safe and happy with Luisa, too. But Luisa's mom said no to Luisa caring for two ferrets. So while Marshmallow was at Luisa's house, Gil, the boy next door, was going to come to Emma's house each day to play with Marmaduke and feed him and clean his cage.

Poor Marmaduke, alone in an empty house. Emma hugged him close to her. She maybe squooshed him too hard, because he shook himself.

"Sorry," she whispered.

Gently, she set him on the floor and looked

4

again at the mess. It was hopeless. She'd read just for a minute. She reached up to the shelf above the window seat for her favorite book, *The Secret Garden*. She kept it there, hidden from her ferrets because they liked to chew on books. Once, Marmaduke had chewed up a super-important book that Emma had stolen—well, borrowed—before she could give it back to its owner. That had caused a terrible uproar.

Emma had read *The Secret Garden* a gazillion times. She turned to the best chapter, the one where the kids discover the secret garden behind a huge wall. It made Emma think of Maine, and the deer path, and her very own tree.

"Emma?" Daddy was calling up the stairs. "How's the packing coming along?"

Emma pretended not to hear. She had just gotten to the good part, where the robin finds the key to the garden.

"Emma?" Daddy called again, a little louder this time. "I'm starting to load the car. Are you finished yet?"

Emma slammed the book closed. "Almost!" she called down.

Big fat lie.

"Tim? How about you? Your things ready?" Daddy called.

"Almost!" Tim called back.

Tim wasn't lying, Emma was sure of it.

Tim was just ten-and-a-half months older than Emma was. He was a little timid and scared of things, not at all like Emma. But he was also super-smart and super-organized and awfully nice, too. He was Emma's best friend. He was sure to have everything packed and ready.

Emma sighed; she might as well get to it. She chased Woof off the bed and swept all her clothes onto the floor. Mom had bought the five kids their own duffel bags, a different color for each person. Emma's was boring, plain old gray. Earlier, she had used Magic Markers to liven it up, drawing red and pink polka dots all over it. It lay on the floor like a huge deflated elephant—an elephant with measles.

Emma began stuffing things into it—books, clothes, sneakers. Her skateboard was on the floor by the bed, and for a minute, she was tempted to put that in, too. But Mom had said no to skateboards in Maine. A really silly rule. Emma slid the skateboard under the bed and continued shoving the rest of her stuff into the bag. It was hard work. She grunted. She shoved some more. She got it all in and then sat on the bag. It collapsed and tumbled over. But the stuff stayed inside. Mostly. Emma moved back to take a careful look.

Marmaduke was checking it out, too. He stuck his nose into the bag, then flattened himself and wriggled his little furry body partway inside.

"Oh, no you don't!" Emma said, and she lifted him out gently. But then she thought . . . *you couldn't see him if he crawled inside . . . he didn't mind closed spaces . . . lots of times he slept inside her pillowcase or her backpack. Could she possibly . . .*

No. She couldn't. It would be wrong to do that.

Except, she wouldn't have to do it. Marmaduke had actually tried to crawl in. All by himself. Just a minute ago. It could happen without her knowing.

Couldn't it?

Chapter Two

A Ferret in a Backpack

It was morning. The kids were packed. The cars were packed. The house was closed up and locked. The whole family was set to go. There was just one thing left to do—*Well*, Emma thought, *maybe two.*

The first was that Daddy had to take a family picture. He did that *every* year before they left for Maine and then took another when they got back. He liked to compare the pictures, to see how they had all changed over the summer, and how tanned and sunny and rested they looked after their vacation.

Nobody changed as much as Daddy, though. In Maine, Daddy didn't shave, and he grew a funny, reddish beard. Emma didn't like the beard much, and she wouldn't kiss him when it got too bushy and scratchy.

Now, while Daddy fiddled with his camera, they all gathered on the porch steps. Mom sat in the middle of the top step, Tim on one side of her, Emma on the other.

On the step below was McClain, Emma's five-year-old sister, hugging her pet cat, Kelley.

Beside McClain were the toddler twins, Ira and Lizzie, along with Annie. The twins weren't quite three years old, but they could say just about everything. They'd learned to talk before they even turned two, and Mom said that once they'd learned, they'd never stopped.

Now Mom put one arm around Emma's shoulder and one around Tim's. She smiled at them. "You all excited?" she asked.

Tim nodded. "I can't wait," he said. "As soon as we get there, I'm setting up my telescope."

Emma nodded, too, but she didn't speak. Her heart was doing odd fluttery things, and she was finding it hard to swallow. Last night, when Luisa and her mom had taken Marshmallow away, it had almost broken Emma's heart. Luisa had Marshmallow snuggled up on her shoulder. And when they had gotten into Luisa's car, Marshmallow hadn't even looked back at Emma to say good-bye. Now Marmaduke was locked up in the house. Alone. The only friend he'd have all summer would be Gil. One visit each day.

"Emma?" Mom said. "You okay? You seem quiet."

"I'm okay," Emma said.

"I'm okay, too!" McClain said. "I'm even more better. I'm happy!"

McClain leaned her head back so it was resting against Emma's knees. Emma put one hand on McClain's mass of curls. McClain could be a big fat pain. Sometimes she had temper tantrums and locked herself in her room and banged things. She was stubborn and threw herself on the ground when she didn't get her way. But she got over it fast. And she was never mean. Emma loved her to pieces.

McClain sat up and hugged Kelley under her chin as if Kelley were just a stuffed animal. That didn't seem to bother Kelley at all.

Emma thought it was totally unfair that Kelley could go to Maine and Marmaduke and Marshmallow couldn't.

Ira and Lizzie both were jumbled up on Annie's lap. They were sticking their little fingers into Annie's mouth, and Annie was pretending to gnaw on them. The little ones were giggling like crazy. Annie was pretending to growl.

Emma sighed. Sometimes she wished she were still a little kid. No worries.

"Okay," Daddy called out at last. "Smile! Say, *broccoli!*"

"Dad-dy!" Ira yelled. "You're s'pposed to say, 'Say cheese.'"

"I am?" Daddy said. "Oh. Okay, say . . . , *mozzarella cheese!*"

"Dad —*dy!*" Lizzie yelled.

"Wait!" McClain shouted. "Woof! Where's Woof?"

At the mention of his name, Woof came galloping around from the back of the house. He looked from one person to the other, as if wondering what was going on. Then, he seemed to figure it out—pictures! He sat himself down right in front of everybody, his head high, his ears pricked up, as if he were posing for a dog-food ad.

"Okay, Woof!" Daddy said. "Say, *liver treats!*"

Woof barked, everybody laughed, and Daddy snapped a bunch of pictures. Then, Mom changed places with Daddy, so he could be in the picture, and she took pictures, too. Finally, it was time to go, and they all got to their feet.

It had already been decided who would go in which car. Tim and the twins would drive with Daddy in the van, along with suitcases and fishing stuff and Woof's beat-up doggie bed and more stuff. McClain and Kelley and the cat carrier and more luggage and pillows would go with Mom in her car. And Annie got Emma and Woof in her little car.

Emma had worked that out last night, and Mom and Daddy had agreed. Annie had been their nanny for less than a year, so she'd never been to the Maine house. The house was hidden from the main road; a rutted path led down to it through the woods. Emma would be able to help with directions once they got close.

Now Mom got in her car. Daddy went to the van. Annie got into her car. All the other kids went scrambling to their seats.

Emma stood perfectly still. Yes? No. Yes. Her heart was beating like crazy. She took a deep breath.

"Daddy!" she yelled. "Daddy, wait! I forgot something. I have to go back in the house."

"Emma!" Daddy said, turning to her. "For heaven's sake! The house is all locked up. I've set the alarms and everything."

"But I have to, Daddy! I forgot my backpack. It's got all my stuff. My books and iPod and . . . and everything."

Daddy sighed and shook his head. "All right, all right," he said. "I'll get it. Where is it?"

"No!" Emma said. "I'll get it. I have to put in one more thing. I mean, I need . . ."

Daddy made a grumpy face and shook his head. But he took out the house keys and went up the steps, Emma following behind. Daddy unlocked the door and turned off the alarm.

"I'll be right down!" Emma said. She raced past him and up the stairs.

In her room, she knelt on the floor in front of Marmaduke's cage. She took the note she had written to Gil out of her pocket. She hadn't been sure she was going to use it. She had written it just in case. She smoothed it out. In huge, black letters, it said:

Dear Gil.

We changed ar minds. We ar taking Marmaduke. We wil pay yu anyway. Wen we get back.

She looked at the words. Some of them were weird looking. She wasn't very good at spelling. But Gil would understand.

She laid the note on the floor, right in front of the cage.

13

Quietly, she opened the cage and gently lifted Marmaduke out. Her backpack was on the floor nearby, where she had set it earlier. She slid Marmaduke inside. He wriggled around, sniffing and snuffling. His eyes, like shiny, black raisins, smiled up at her. He liked her backpack.

"Okay, Marmaduke," she whispered. "I'm going to close it up now. But just for a minute. I'll open it as soon as we get in the car. You ready?"

"Emma!" Daddy called. "What's taking so long? We're waiting."

She heard his footsteps on the stairs.

"Don't come up!" she yelled. "I'm coming, I'm coming!"

She quickly zipped the backpack. All the way to the top. She picked it up and held it close. She raced down the stairs. "I have it, I have it," she said. She ran past Daddy and outside to Annie's car.

She did have it. Him. Marmaduke.

And when Mom and Daddy found out, they were going to kill her.

Chapter Three
Woof Throws Up

Emma climbed into the backseat of Annie's car, holding the backpack close to her chest. Woof leaped onto the seat beside her.

Emma knew she had to ride in back because of air bags. That was just fine with her. It was easier to hide Marmaduke from Annie that way.

Annie was super-wonderful. She came from Ireland and talked funny sometimes, saying things like *knickers* instead of *underwear*, and *loo* instead of *bathroom*. She was young and pretty and sweet and kind. She adored all the kids, and once in a while, she even got herself into trouble along with them. She also loved Marshmallow and Marmaduke almost as much as Emma did. Still, Emma was pretty sure Annie wouldn't approve of Marmaduke being smuggled off to Maine. So it was best for Annie if she just didn't know.

15

Emma settled into the seat, still hugging her backpack, trying to slow her breathing. Her heart had been beating wildly, and she was all sweaty.

"Ready?" Annie said, looking over the seat at Emma.

"Ready!" Emma said. "Let's go."

Annie frowned a little. "You okay, me dear? You're all red in the face. Are you feeling all right?"

Emma nodded. "I'm okay. I'm fine. Let's go."

"You sure?"

"I'm sure! I'm fine."

Well, not exactly fine. Marmaduke had begun wriggling about inside the backpack. Annie would surely notice. Emma started to squeeze him tighter but was scared she'd squash him. She bent and set the backpack gently on the floor.

"Emma?" Annie said.

"What?"

"Emma, dear, you don't have your skateboard in that backpack, now, do you?" Annie asked. "You know what your mum said about that."

Emma sat up straight. She found her seat belt and snapped it on. "No!" she said. "I don't have my skateboard. Or my RipStik. Just stuff. Now, come on. The others will get there ahead of us."

"Promise me?" Annie said.

"Promise!" Emma said.

"Then, we're on our way," Annie said, smiling.

Emma let out a huge sigh of relief.

As soon as Annie backed the car out of the driveway and turned down the street, Emma leaned over again. She began unzipping the backpack slowly, a tiny bit at a time—not too fast or too far, or Marmaduke would come popping out.

"Want to play the license plate game?" Annie asked.

"In a minute," Emma answered. She was still bent over. She inched the zipper down farther, and Marmaduke's little nose poked out.

Right away, Woof jumped down and shoved his head into the backpack. His little, stubby tail began wagging like crazy as he sniffed hello to Marmaduke.

Emma pushed him away. "Go away, Woof," she muttered. She didn't need Woof to start yapping hello at Marmaduke.

Woof didn't go away. He kept right on sniffing. Suddenly, Emma heard Woof's tummy rumbling, and then there was kind of an awful smell.

"Yuck!" she yelled.

"What's wrong?" Annie asked.

"Woof!" Emma said. "I forgot. He needs a window open. He gets carsick on long trips. I gave him his carsick pill this morning, but he has to stick his head out, remember?"

"Oh, indeed," Annie said. "But we're turning onto the highway now, and it's sure to be a bit noisy with the window down. We won't be able to hear each other for our license plate game."

"That's all right," Emma said. "Otherwise, he throws up."

Emma pushed the button, and her window slid down. Woof scrambled up onto the seat and stuck his head out. His ears flapped in the wind. His mouth was open as if he were smiling.

Good. He was out of the way for a while.

Emma turned back to Marmaduke, inching the zipper down until Marmaduke's whole head popped out. He looked around—not that there was much to see from down where he was.

Emma patted his sweet, little head. Then she took a deep breath and sat back. She put in her earphones and turned on her iPod. Perfect. She kept a careful watch on Marmaduke to be sure his whole body didn't pop out, but he seemed to be settling down to take a nap. The car often lulled him to sleep.

They drove a ways with neither Emma nor Annie saying much, since they would have had to yell to hear each other because of the open window and the earphones. After a while, Annie called back, "You okay back there?"

"We're okay," Emma answered. "How far have we gone?"

"Oh, maybe . . . about a hundred kilometers."

"What's that in miles?" Emma asked.

"Oh," Annie said, laughing. "I always forget. I still think I'm in Ireland sometimes. It's close to sixty miles, I guess."

Good. Too far to turn back. Not that Annie would do that. Still, you could never tell.

"Can you close the window for a minute?" Annie yelled.

Emma leaned over and pulled Woof back inside. She pushed the button and the window slid up. The car got very quiet.

"That's better," Annie said. "Are you ready to stop for a bite of lunch yet?"

"Lunch?" Emma said. She hadn't even thought that they'd stop to eat! She couldn't go into a restaurant and leave Marmaduke in the backpack all alone. The car would get too hot. He'd suffocate. And if she let him out of the backpack, he'd tear the car to pieces.

"No!" she said. "No. I don't want to stop at all. I want to get there. Let's just keep driving!"

"Oh, we'll have to stop eventually," Annie said. "Woof is going to need a rest stop pretty soon. And besides, you must be hungry. I know I am. We still have over two hours to go."

Now what?

Woof had crept closer to Emma and buried his head in her lap. His ears were kind of droopy again. Emma rubbed that pointy part on the top of his head. He shook his head and his ears flapped. Then he burrowed deep into Emma's lap again. He breathed a big, long sigh.

"Woof, you can hold it till we get there," Emma said. "Can't you, Woof?"

Woof didn't answer. He just breathed hard. And then, he made a kind of worrisome sound. He gagged. And gagged again. And then he threw up. Right into Emma's lap.

And down on the floor.

Into the backpack, too.

Chapter Four
Oh, Emma!

"*Oh, Emma!*"

Annie kept shaking her head and muttering those two words over and over again as she tried to clean up Emma. And Woof. And Marmaduke. And the backpack and the floor of the car.

Well, it's not like I threw up, Emma said. But she just said it inside her head. She knew Annie wasn't muttering and shaking her head over throw-up. She knew exactly what Annie was mumbling about. Still, Annie didn't ask how Marmaduke had ended up in the backpack. Not yet. And Emma didn't offer to tell.

Eventually, they were all more or less cleaned up. Before they got back onto the highway, though, Annie insisted on a detour. She said they needed to find a pet store and buy a cage and food and a water bottle for Marmaduke. Marmaduke would need all that in Maine, anyway, Annie said, and he sure couldn't ride the rest of the way in a smelly backpack.

While they were in the pet store—Emma holding Marmaduke tightly under her sweatshirt because she couldn't leave him in the car—Emma noticed that there were little floats for sale. She wondered what kind of pet they were for—surely not for cats. Cats hated water. Ferrets, maybe? Marmaduke liked water. He was always trying to creep into the shower with her. She wondered if he'd like sailing in the lake. But she knew she didn't dare ask Annie to buy him a float.

As it was, Annie was spending a whole lot of money on Marmaduke. Emma saw the price on the cage. It was over seventy-five dollars!

"Annie?" Emma said, still holding tight to Marmaduke, as Annie paid. "I'll pay you back. I have some money."

"We'll talk about it later," Annie said.

"But I really do have money," Emma said. "I've been saving up for a soccer net in the backyard. I don't have it with me, but I can give it to you when we get home. I have more than fifty dollars. Honest."

"It's all right, me dear," Annie said. "We'll talk

later. You and I have many things to talk about. Now come, we need to get back to the car and get Marmaduke into his cage. If he squirms out of your arms, we're in fine trouble."

"He wouldn't do that," Emma said. She ducked inside her sweatshirt and buried her face in Marmaduke's fur. "Would you, Marmaduke?"

Marmaduke stuck his little face up and Emma kissed him.

It took a while, but finally they were on the highway again, headed for the lake. Marmaduke was in his brand-new cage on the seat beside Emma, happily looking around. The cage was big and took up a lot of space. Emma had seen another one in the store called a ferret mansion. She'd wanted that one for Marmaduke but it had cost two hundred dollars. As it was, she was feeling pretty awful about all the money Annie had spent.

Now Woof had stuck his head out the window, smiling and panting. Annie was driving and even humming a little to herself. Things were better.

Except not really. The closer they got to Maine, the more Emma worried. She had broken all kinds of rules and been really dishonest, too. Would Mom and Daddy understand that she just couldn't bear to leave Marmaduke alone? She hadn't meant to be bad. She really hadn't. But it had broken her heart when Luisa had gone off with Marshmallow last night. Emma just couldn't leave Marmaduke behind, too.

Annie hadn't yet asked about how Marmaduke had happened to come along. But she would. Emma knew that, and she had already planned what to say: It wasn't her fault that Marmaduke had snuck into the backpack. Everybody knew how Marmaduke loved getting into tight places. Like the fold-up couch.

Yes, but it's a lie. Marmaduke didn't sneak in.

It's not a bad lie, though.

It's still a lie.

But it's not a hurt-somebody kind of lie.

Lie, lie, lie.

Oh, hush up.

That was the way all of Emma's arguments with herself ended. What to do? Emma hated lying, even though sometimes she had to. But she especially hated lying to Annie.

"Annie?" Emma said at last. She leaned over the seat, as far as her seat belt would allow, so that Annie could hear her. "Are you mad at me, Annie?"

"No, me dear," Annie said. "Never mad at you."

"But you think I shouldn't have . . . let Marmaduke come?"

"I think you could have made a better choice."

"I didn't bring my skateboard," Emma said.

Annie laughed. "That probably would have been better."

"Do you think Mom and Daddy are going to be mad?"

"I do."

"I do, too," Emma said. "They'll kill me. Annie, what if . . . what if I just say that Marmaduke snuck into my backpack?"

Annie was quiet for a minute. And then she said, "Did he?"

"No," Emma answered.

"Oh," Annie said.

Emma leaned back in her seat. She stared down at her fingernails. She nibbled on her thumb. She thought about all the fun things she did year after year in Maine. And how maybe now she wouldn't be allowed to do any of them. She'd be grounded for sure.

After a while, she leaned forward again. "Annie?" she said. "Okay. Can we keep him a secret just till tonight? Can we leave him in the car, maybe back under the trees so he doesn't get hot? And no one sees him? Just till tonight, please?"

"We could," Annie said slowly. "But you know

what, Emma? Putting things off doesn't make anything easier. Sometimes, it even makes everything harder."

"I know," Emma said. "But I have to do some stuff first. Before I tell."

"Like what?" Annie asked.

"Well," Emma said. "First, I need to see Max. Then I need to climb my tree, my special tree. And I want to see the deer and the deer path. The deer path goes right under my tree. And I have to swim in the lake, just once."

"And you have to do all that before you tell about Marmaduke?" Annie asked, laughing.

"Yes!" Emma said. "Because once they find out, I'm going to be grounded. For the rest of the summer, probably. Maybe even for the rest of my life."

Again, Annie laughed. "I don't think for the rest of your life," she said.

"Till I'm thirty or forty, anyway," Emma said. "But at least I'll have Marmaduke to play with. Do you think ferrets live that long?"

"I think they live a long time," Annie said.

"You know what else, Annie?" Emma said. "I saw some floats back in the pet store. You know how Marmaduke likes water, how he likes to get in the shower with me? Maybe I can save up some money and buy him a float. After I pay you back, I mean."

"And set him out there in the *lake*?" Annie said. She sounded a little horrified.

"Why not?" Emma said.

"Me dear! He could fall off. And drown!" Annie said.

"Not if I make him drown-proof. Like they tell us in swimming class. So I'll teach him to swim. In the bathtub. What do you think of that?"

"Oh, Emma!" Annie said.

Chapter Five
The Haunted House

They were there. They were finally there! At the lake house, Emma's favorite place in the whole, wide world. It had been Daddy's summer house when he was a little boy, and the family had been going there every summer for years. A long time ago, Grandma and Grandpa had lived there, but then they had moved to Colorado. They liked Colorado so much—even in the summer—that they hardly ever came to the lake house anymore.

The house was on a little rise, shaded by trees, with porches on all sides so you could watch the sunrise and the sunset, too. Beyond the house, down the rickety, wooden steps to the dock, the lake glittered in the sun. It was so bright that Emma had to shield her eyes. The raft that they always swam to bobbed gently up and down, and Emma saw a duck sitting right in the middle of it, sunning

28

himself. Above, pine trees swayed, and birds twittered and flitted about, showing flashes of red and brown and blue.

Emma breathed in deeply. The smell of the pines was the smell of Maine. After a whole, long winter, she was here at last.

She raced from the car to the house, Woof galloping along behind her, Annie following. On the screened-in porch, the whole family was already gathered. The little kids were pushing Matchbox cars around the floor. The minute they saw Annie, they scrambled to their feet and began jumping up and down, yelling, "Annie, Annie, Annie!"

McClain threw open the door. "Emma, Annie!" she yelled. "I saw chipmunks! Bunches of chipmunks."

Tim and Daddy were already setting up Tim's telescope in one corner. Max and Uncle Max and Auntie Liz were there, too. They were helping Mom set out chairs and cushions.

"Emma!" Max yelled when Emma came bursting onto the porch.

"Max!" Emma yelled back.

Uncle Max turned. He grabbed Emma in a hug and lifted her off the floor. "Look at you!" he said. "Look how big you've gotten!" He grinned at her, then set her down and bent to ruffle Woof's ears.

Everyone began talking at once, asking why Emma and Annie had taken so long to get there and how was traffic and all that. Auntie Liz hugged Emma and smiled down at her. "You get more beautiful each time I see you," she said softly. "I've missed you."

"*I've missed you!*" Emma said. It was true. She liked Auntie Liz. A lot.

Max crossed the porch to Emma. He shoved her with his shoulder. She stumbled back. He stepped on her foot. On purpose.

Emma shoved him back. She wasn't mad. She knew boys did stuff like that when they liked you. They couldn't help it.

"Want to go to the woods?" Max asked.

"Yes!" Emma said. She glanced at Annie.

Annie smiled and nodded.

Emma was pretty sure she knew what Annie was thinking—that this was Emma's last chance to be free. Before *big trouble*.

"Listen for the gong!" Daddy said. He meant the big bell that hung outside the porch. When it rang, it meant that all the kids had to come home, usually for dinner.

"And don't go inside that house," Uncle Max said, looking right at Max.

"I won't," Max said.

Emma and Max jumped down off the porch. Before they'd gone even a step, though, Emma thought of something and turned back. "Tim?" she called through the screen. "Do you want to come, too?"

Tim used to run in the woods with Emma and Max. But then last summer, somebody had said they'd seen a bear digging around under an old rotted tree stump. Ever since, Tim had said no when Emma had asked him to come along. Emma was pretty sure it was because of bears, even though Tim said it wasn't. Still, she didn't want to leave him behind, just in case he'd changed his mind since last summer. Sometimes, he was too shy to ask.

"Thanks," he said, "but I want to set up my telescope."

"Okay!" Emma said.

She and Max took off, running—Emma, running because she had been cooped up in the car for so long, and Max, trying to keep up. Emma could hear him panting. She could also hear a clicking sound, as if stuff was jingling around in his pockets. She remembered how he collected things, shells or rocks or bottle caps or even just string. Auntie Liz called him a pack rat.

After a little while, they slowed to a walk and the

jingling sound stopped. "What are you collecting now?" Emma asked.

"Just stuff. I found a bear tooth!" Max said.

"For real?" Emma said. "Can I see?"

"Sure," Max said. He dug in his pocket and brought out a handful of rocks and acorns and screws and something that looked a little yucky, like maybe it was a dead toad. After a moment, he found what he was looking for, wiped it off on his shirt, and handed it to Emma.

It was small, about the size of Emma's thumb, yellow and curved and kind of pointy on one end. It was heavy, too. Emma didn't think it was a bear tooth, though. It looked just like a seashell—a seashell with barnacles stuck to it. She was pretty sure, though, that Max would feel bad if she said that. So she just said, "Cool."

She handed it back to him. And then she asked, "What house was your dad talking about when he said, 'Don't go inside that house'?"

"You know, the haunted house," Max said.

"The haunted house?" Emma asked. "It's all falling down."

"Not anymore," Max said. "Somebody bought it. They've added so much to it, it's crazy. They're putting in tennis courts and a swimming pool and a barn with a gold eagle on top and everything."

"Wow!" Emma said. "I love tennis. Maybe they'll invite us over to play. Or swim in their pool."

"Uh-uh," Max said. "There are no kids. Just old people, Mr. and Mrs. Thompson. I don't think they want kids around. They haven't moved in yet, but Dad met them in town. Mr. Thompson said they're putting a big, wire fence all the way around the property."

Emma frowned. "To keep kids out?"

"No, silly," Max said. "To keep deer out."

"Weird. What would they want to do that for?" Emma said.

"Maybe they hate deer. Or else they don't want the deer to eat their gardens. I don't know," Max said. "Anyway, Dad says they have more money than brains. Mom said that's not nice, but it's probably true."

By then, Emma and Max had reached the place where the deer path split—one part going up toward the Thomson's house, the other heading down to the lake. And right where the path divided was Emma's tree, her beautiful, wide-spreading red oak tree.

"My tree!" Emma said. "Oh stop. Look, my tree!"

Max didn't stop. "Come on," he said. "I want to see if the builders have started on the roof." He turned onto the path to the house.

Good thing. Because, if Max were watching, Emma would have felt a little silly doing what she was about to do. She put her arms around her tree and leaned against it. "Hi, tree," she whispered.

A breeze blew, and for a moment, the tree seemed to embrace her. Its long branches grew thick and close, sweeping almost to the ground, closing her in. She stood for a moment, breathing in the happiness, just as she had breathed in the scent of the pines.

Something was weird, though. Someone had tied a big, yellow ribbon around the tree trunk. Emma remembered a song she'd heard about tying a yellow ribbon around an old oak tree. She wondered if the ribbon meant that the Thompsons liked her tree. Maybe they weren't so bad after all. Even if Max had said they wouldn't let her on their tennis courts or in their pool. Even if they didn't like deer. They liked trees, her tree.

"Emma!" Max called. "Come on."

"Coming!" she called. To her tree, she whispered, "I'll be back."

She ran along the path to where Max was standing. The old, haunted house was in front of them, gray and sad looking, leaning toward the earth. But right alongside it loomed the walls of another house. The second house wasn't finished; it was just a frame with open spaces where windows and doors were going to be. But it was huge. Enormous. It had a second floor, and even a third, but no roof yet, so it stood open to the sky. It was the biggest house Emma had ever seen—or, at least, the biggest almost-house in Maine.

"Maybe it's going to be a hotel?" Emma said.

"Nope," Max said. "I told you. It's a house."

Emma moved closer so she could see more, Max right beside her. Inside were partitions marking off rooms, many rooms. There was no stairway to the upper floors yet, just a hole where a stairway would go. A ladder stretched from the ground floor up to the hole above.

"Let's go in," Max said. "Want to?"

Well, Emma wasn't going to say, "Your dad said not to." And nobody had told *her* she couldn't.

"Sure," she said.

They stepped through one of the doorway openings. Emma raced for the ladder, but Max got there first. He scooted up the ladder and disappeared onto the second floor, agile as a monkey. Emma raced up behind him. Once there, they both straightened up and looked around.

The part of the house where they stood faced the lake. Through the trees, Emma could catch a glimmer of sun shining off the water. There were trees all around, waving lazily in the breeze. Off to one side, she could even see *her* tree—at least, she thought it was hers, because of the yellow ribbon. But then she noticed other trees, many trees, also wearing yellow ribbons.

"That's weird," Emma said. "Why do they put ribbons on the trees?"

"Those are the trees they're going to cut down."

"*What?*" Emma said.

"Cut them down," Max said. "That's what they said. The trees are spoiling their view of the lake. Mr. Thompson told my dad."

"They're *cutting* those trees *down?*" Emma said. Max nodded.

"No!" Emma whispered. For a minute, an awful, sad, choked-up feeling welled up inside her. She felt as if she would burst into tears. Her tree? Her tree that she dreamed about all year long? All those trees? They couldn't. They shouldn't!

But the sadness lasted just a moment. Because she was suddenly mad. Mad!

"Oh, no they're not," Emma said. "They are not cutting down those trees. Not *my* tree. *No way.*"

Chapter Six

Out on the Porch

Nighttime came. Dark, black night. Emma lay in bed, very still, listening. Waiting. Waiting. She had told Annie that after everyone had gone to bed—the little kids and even Tim—and Mom and Daddy were by themselves, that's when she would tell about Marmaduke. She'd tell them that he was there, right outside in the car.

The little kids had long ago been tucked in to sleep. Tim had finally closed down his telescope for the night. Even Annie had gone to her room in the loft.

And Emma lay in bed, waiting. Waiting.

She wasn't waiting to talk to Mom and Daddy, though. She was waiting for them to go to bed and go to sleep.

She had a plan. In the morning, she and Max were going to cut the yellow ribbon off her tree and maybe off other trees, too. Probably the Thompsons had no idea which trees they had marked to be cut down, anyway. Then, when that was done—when her tree was safe—then Emma would confess about Marmaduke. It was only for one more day, not even a whole day, just half a day, just tomorrow morning. So it wasn't really bad. Emma figured Annie would understand that. By tomorrow at this time, she'd have told the truth. She'd be grounded. But her tree would be saved.

What Emma needed to do now, though—if Mom and Daddy would ever go to bed!—was to smuggle Marmaduke over to Max's house and hide him in Max's room. She couldn't leave him in the car all night and half of tomorrow. He'd get hot and hungry and lonely, and Annie's car would begin to smell. Max said his mom never came into his room because it was such a mess—also because Max had a pet snake, Flamester. Auntie Liz didn't think much of snakes. It would be a perfect hiding place for Marmaduke for the day.

Beside Emma's bed, Woof turned himself 'round and 'round, then settled down to sleep in a big circle of fur and warmth. Kelley, McClain's cat, had abandoned McClain and for some reason had decided to share Emma's bed for the night. Now

Kelley was sleeping heavily right on top of Emma's feet.

Emma hoped Marmaduke was sleeping, too. She'd be rescuing him soon. Except that Mom and Daddy were *still* awake. Emma could hear the soft murmur of their voices in the big center room, and the click of their coffee cups, and an occasional laugh. Outside, crickets and night creatures began chirping. A bullfrog called loudly, announcing he was king of the lake.

It was very, very dark outside, the house buried in the woods, not at all like back home. Here there were no street lights, no car lights, just black, black night with stars that came down so low they seemed to sit right on top of the lake. All the rooms, even the bedrooms, were on one floor, except for the little loft over the living room where Annie slept. Emma loved the loft, but she liked her room even better. It was at the front of the house, with windows facing the lake, right next to the screened-in porch.

It felt like forever that Emma lay there, waiting, waiting, waiting for Mom and Daddy to go to bed. To keep from falling asleep, she tried to recite every state in the United States alphabetically. She was stuck on the *M* states. Maryland, Massachusetts,

Michigan, Minnesota, Mississippi, Missouri, Montana. What else? She had left one out. She knew there were eight, but she could think of only seven.

And then—from the crack under her door, Emma saw the lights go out in the big center room. She heard Mom and Daddy go down the hall to their bedroom in the back.

Oh! *Maine*! It was Maine that she'd forgotten. How very, very silly of her.

No more sounds. No more lights.

Emma sat up. She crept out of bed, careful not to make any noise. It was cold! She dug around at the foot of the bed and found her sweatshirt. She pulled it on.

Tim had given her a Mickey Mouse watch with a light-up face for her birthday. She looked at it. Eleven o'clock. She'd have to wait another whole hour. She and Max had agreed to wait till midnight to be sure that the grown-ups in both houses were asleep.

Emma decided to go outside right now and get Marmaduke. He'd be happy to be cuddled for a while, and it would help her stay awake till midnight. As soon as she opened her bedroom door, Woof scrambled to his feet. He followed her

40

from her room to the big room and then out to the porch.

"Shh!" Emma said. Very quietly, she closed the house door behind her. She patted Woof's head. "You wait here on the porch," she whispered. "I'll be back in a minute."

She opened the outside porch door and went down the few steps to the ground. Then she followed the path to where Annie's car was parked under the trees. The path made crunchy sounds under her bare feet so she moved over onto the grass. The grass was wet and cold, but a nice cold. When she got to the car and opened the door, the little light came on inside. There was Marmaduke, sound asleep in his cage.

"Hey, buddy," Emma whispered. "Want to come with me?"

Marmaduke raised his head. He looked up at Emma. He smiled. He seemed to smile.

Emma lifted him out. She tucked him close against her side, then took the cage and his food out, too. The cage wasn't heavy, but it was big and awkward. She wouldn't carry Marmaduke inside it, because he might get jounced around too much and get hurt. Instead, she put the food inside the cage, snapped the cage closed, and held it in one hand; with her other arm, she pressed Marmaduke close to her. Quietly, she pushed the car door closed with her hip. When it clicked shut, Emma winced. It sounded extra loud in the silence.

She stood still for a minute. Had anyone heard? She looked around, holding her breath. No. No lights had come on inside the house. Breathing a big sigh of relief, she headed back toward the house. Again, she walked on the grass, trying to avoid branches, not moving any pebbles.

When she reached the house, she set the cage on the grass by the steps. Then she opened the door, closed it quietly behind her, and tiptoed across the porch. She settled herself and Marmaduke on the big, double swing. She patted the seat beside her and Woof leaped up, sending the swing gyrating madly for a moment. Emma pulled the quilt resting on the back of the swing around her, sharing it with Woof and Marmaduke, too. Marmaduke made himself extra cozy by crawling up inside Emma's sweatshirt.

Emma smiled. She leaned her head against the back of the swing. With one toe against the floor, she pushed, rocking herself and Woof and Marmaduke just a little. It was so peaceful here. She could hear a mockingbird—the only bird that sang at night,

Daddy had told her—calling out his lonely song. She may have even fallen asleep or begun to fall asleep when . . . the door behind her creaked.

Emma bolted upright. She sucked in her breath. She turned. The door to the inside, the house door, was opening slowly.

Daddy!

Chapter Seven
Hiding Marmaduke

"You scared me," Emma said. Her heart had begun hammering wildly. She folded both arms across herself, squeezing Marmaduke tight against her, and tugged the quilt a little higher.

"I'm sorry. I didn't mean to," Daddy said. "I thought I heard you out here. I wondered if maybe you'd like company."

"No, no. I don't," Emma said. "I mean . . . I just like it out here. Alone." Her throat was so tight, she could hardly speak.

"Are you all right?" Daddy asked. "Couldn't sleep?"

"I'm fine!" Emma said.

Daddy came over to the swing. "Scooch over a little," he said. "Come on, Woof, make room."

Woof jumped down to the floor. He turned 'round and 'round, then curled up beneath Emma's feet.

44

"No!" Emma said. "I'm going back to bed now."

"Can't I join you for just a minute?" Daddy said.

What could she say? What could she do? Nothing. She was trapped. She moved over a tiny bit.

Daddy put an arm around her shoulders. "When I heard you out here, it made me think of something," he said. "You might not believe this, but when I was your age, I did exactly what you are doing right now."

Emma squeezed Marmaduke closer.

Oh, no you didn't, she thought.

"I used to come out on this porch on summer nights," Daddy said. "Just me, alone in the dark, after everyone else was asleep. I loved it here at night in the quiet and the dark." He smoothed Emma's hair. "You do, too, don't you?"

"I love the trees," Emma whispered. "And the lake. And being in the dark. *Alone*."

Marmaduke was wriggling around, as though he needed air. Any minute now, he'd poke his nose up, right out of the neck of her sweatshirt.

"But you know what?" Daddy went on. "Know what I did one night—out here in the dark? I went swimming in the lake."

Emma twisted around to look up at him. "Alone? You should never go swimming alone!" She had learned that in her swimming classes. "*Alone in the dark*? That was stupid!" she said.

"It was," Daddy said, turning to look out over the lake as if he were remembering. "Really stupid. I never did it again."

Emma shook her head.

Marmaduke did, too.

He had poked his nose up and out of the neck of her sweatshirt and was looking this way and that.

Emma whipped around, turning completely away from Daddy. She fumbled for the quilt. She tugged it over Marmaduke's head and right up to her own chin.

"You okay, honey?" Daddy asked. "You have a chill?"

"No! I'm fine. I just want to be . . . alone."

Daddy stood up. "Okay," he said, "I understand. Good night, sweetie." He bent and kissed the top of her head.

Good night! Good-bye! Except then Emma felt guilty. "Daddy?" she said. "Daddy, it's not *you*. It's not that I don't like being with you. It's . . ."

"It's all right," Daddy said. "I understand. I really do. Good night, sweetie."

"'Night, Daddy," Emma said.

The door closed. Emma uncovered Marmaduke's

head. She leaned back against the swing. She buried her toes in Woof's warm fur. She closed her eyes and breathed deeply. Daddy didn't *really* understand.

He really, really didn't.

She buried her face in Marmaduke's warm fur.

Thank goodness.

Chapter Eight

Through the Dark, Dark Woods

Max was asleep! His whole house was asleep. Pitch dark, not a single light burning. Emma stood on the porch, so mad.

She had walked all the way over to Max's house carrying the cage and the food, and Marmaduke. It hadn't been easy, either! She'd been kind of scared, too, so she'd been singing to keep up her courage. It was because of bears. Emma figured that if bears were scared of people—Daddy said they were—then they'd stay away if they heard her singing. She didn't sing really loudly, not loudly enough to wake up anyone in the nearby houses, just loud enough for a bear to hear if it were hanging around. Also, she knew she didn't have a great singing voice. When her second-grade class had had a songfest last year, Emma's teacher had suggested that instead of singing, Emma might want to play the triangle.

She had brought along a flashlight for the walk, holding it clumsily against the cage handle, but even so, once she had tripped and stubbed her toe, almost dropping Marmaduke. She'd also been startled to pieces when a creature—she thought maybe it was a skunk—appeared on the path in front of her. She stood very still, hardly even breathing, till it crept off into the bushes. Emma and Woof had met with a skunk one time, and it hadn't worked out at all. And now, here she was, standing on the porch of Max's house. And where was Max? He must be sound asleep. And it had been his idea that they wait till midnight.

Emma set the cage on the porch floor. She gently slid Marmaduke down inside, then carefully closed and locked the top. "I'll be back in a minute," she whispered to him. "Don't be scared."

She stepped off the porch and circled the house to the back, keeping the flashlight pointed to the ground. She'd been to this house a zillion times, and she knew just where Max's room was—on the ground floor, just like hers, only his was in the back. She pushed her way through the shrubs that grew up close to the house, then stood on tiptoe and peeked in.

She shone the flashlight inside. She could just make out the bed. And a lump in the bed. Max.

The window was open. She could climb in—but no—there was a screen. She would have to lift the screen out. She tugged at it, trying to push it up. It didn't budge.

She leaned in close, pressing her nose against the screen. "Max!" she called quietly. "Max! Wake up." She tried shining the flashlight right in his face, but his head was buried in the pillow.

"Max?"

He didn't even move.

"Max!" she called, just a little louder. "It's me. Emma."

Still nothing. If she called any louder, she'd wake up the whole house. What to do? She looked around. There was a garden hose near her feet, coiled up like a snake. She could spray it through the window onto his bed. That would wake him up.

Yeah, but it would make a gigantic mess, too.

And then she had a better idea. Maybe the house wasn't locked. Mom and Daddy didn't lock up the lake house the way they locked up the house in town. The same with the cans, luckily. Earlier she'd heard them talking about how safe they felt here. Maybe Uncle Max and Auntie Liz didn't lock up, either.

Emma made a face at Max, even though she knew he couldn't see her. She pushed her way back through the bushes, circled the house, and tiptoed up onto the porch. Carefully, she turned the doorknob of the house door.

Yes! It opened! Just like that.

Silently, she crept inside, leaving Marmaduke in his cage outside. She waited for her eyes to adjust to the dark. She didn't think it would be good to use her flashlight now, in case the light awakened someone. After a minute, she began walking across the main room, her hands out in front of her. Yes, there was the big table. The little upright piano. The circle of chairs. The big sofa.

Straight ahead was the hall to the bedrooms in back. She held her breath. She'd have to go past the door to Uncle Max and Auntie Liz's room. Did they sleep with their door open? Or closed?

Emma tiptoed down the hall, passing two closed doors. A tiny night-light of some sort was glowing near the bathroom, and she used that to guide herself. Max's room was right beside the bathroom. Hugging the wall, she inched her way along.

Boards squeaked under her feet. She stopped. Held her breath. Uncle Max snored from behind a closed door off to her left. Quickly, she scurried the rest of the way down the hall and into Max's room.

She shut the door behind her. Safe! She went over to Max's bed.

"Max!" she said, plopping down beside him. She turned on his bedside lamp. "Wake up, you dodo-head! You were supposed to be outside, waiting."

Max sat up with a start. Emma could see that he was fully dressed, wearing those shorts with all the pockets. She wondered if he still had his bear tooth and the dead toad in there.

"I'm awake, I'm awake," he said. "I was just waiting for Emma. We were going to look for bear teeth and . . ."

And then he fell back onto the bed again—sound asleep.

Emma grabbed his arm and pulled him upright. "Wake up!" she whispered. "Come on! We're not going to look for bear teeth. Or anything else. We're going to hide Marmaduke. And you were supposed to be out on the porch."

"Oh. Sorry." He blinked at her. "What time is it?"

"I don't know. Late. Midnight or something," Emma said. "That's what you said, come at midnight. Now hurry up. We have to bring Marmaduke inside."

"Why?" He slumped back against the pillow.

Emma let out a huffy breath. "Would you please wake up?"

"Okay. Okay." He rubbed his eyes and sat up.

"Oh," he said. "I was supposed to . . . oh . . . I guess I fell asleep."

"You did," Emma said. "Now, come on. Show me where we can put Marmaduke's cage. I left him out on the porch."

"Why?" Max said again.

"Because it was pitch dark in this house, silly!" Emma said. "And because I didn't want to bump into something and—"

"Okay, okay," Max said. "I'm sorry."

He slid off the bed. His crazy red hair was standing up in weird little spikes all over one side of his head. The other side was flattened out. He ran his hands through his hair, making it even more crazy. It reminded Emma of the doll that McClain sometimes carried around by its hair.

"Show me where you're putting him," Emma said again. "And where's your snake and his cage and stuff?"

Max pointed to the glass aquarium on his dresser. "Flamester's over there. Don't worry. He won't bother Marmaduke."

"I'm not worried about Marmaduke," Emma said. "It's Flamester. You know ferrets eat snakes. Well, some ferrets do. Not that Marmaduke would. But, still. If they got together, that could be the end of Flamester."

"Right!" Max said. He looked around the room, seeming still half-asleep. "Oh, okay," he said. "Marmaduke can go over there." He pointed.

He kind of stumbled to the corner of his room where the closet was. He slid one of the doors to the side.

"See?" he said. "In the back."

Emma looked. The closet was crammed full. Boxes were filled to overflowing with all sorts of stuff: horseshoe crabs and seashells, rocks, dog-eared books. There was even a crate of old stuffed animals.

"In *there*?" she said. "There's not an inch of room."

"Is, too!" Max said. He began sweeping stuff off to one side. A jar of acorns tipped over, and the contents went skittering across the floor in all directions. It sounded like rain falling.

"Hope nobody heard that," Emma whispered.

Max straightened up. "They didn't. Don't worry. Now, there! Marmaduke's cage can go right there. I'll take good care of him. I'll feed him and even clean his cage in the morning if you want me to."

"Okay," Emma said. "Thanks." She couldn't help thinking, though, that he didn't know what he'd gotten himself into. The cage would be really

54

smelly by morning.

And then, Emma thought of something. "Uh-oh," she said. "When you clean his cage, you have to carry the mess outside. And hide it in the trash. Or your mom will know. And don't close the closet door! Marmaduke will get scared. And lonely."

"I won't!" Max said. "I'll leave it open so he can look around and stuff. But if Mom decides to come in—and you know she won't—but just in case she does, I'll just slide the closet door closed."

Emma nodded. It was a good plan. If Auntie Liz did peek in, she'd never see anything, because the closet was sort of behind the bedroom door. And the cage would be hidden deep inside it.

But Auntie Liz did peek in. In fact, right that very second, she was peeking in! Well, more than peeking. She was standing in the doorway, staring at them.

Chapter Nine
Moths!

For one instant, Emma thought of diving under the bed. But too late.

"*What* are you two up to?" Auntie Liz asked.

Emma looked at Max. Max looked at Emma.

"I couldn't sleep," Emma said.

"Me, either," Max said.

"How'd you get here?" Auntie Liz said, frowning at Emma.

"I . . . just walked," Emma said.

"In the *dark*?"

"It's not that dark," Emma said. But it was. "I guess I'll go home now."

She started toward the door, sidling around Auntie Liz. She sent a look to Max, reminding him about Marmaduke. *On the porch.* She mouthed the words at him.

"Emma, no!" Auntie Liz said. "I don't want you

walking home alone at this hour."

"Why not?" Emma said. "There are no bears. You know that. It's just a rumor about bears. Besides, we're only like three houses away."

Auntie Liz made a kind of snorting sound. "Three houses, yes, with half a mile between them."

"You're exaggerating!" Emma said.

Auntie Liz laughed. "I am," she said. "But *you* are being a rascal."

"I'll go with her!" Max said.

"No, you won't!" Emma said, glaring at him. "I'm fine. You're making a big deal out of this! We're right next door practically!"

"Okay," Auntie Liz said. "Okay. Go on home. I'll put on the porch lights. That will light the path at least part of the way."

"No!" Emma said. "Don't! I have my flashlight. Look!" She held it up.

Auntie Liz shook her head. "I don't care. I'm turning on the porch light."

If you turn on the light, you'll see Marmaduke, thought Emma.

"But you can't!" Emma said. "The lights attract—moths! Zillions of them. They swarm around lights. You know I'm scared of moths."

"You? Scared of moths? Since when?"

"Since this year. I am very, very scared of moths."

Auntie Liz frowned at Emma. She tilted her head to one side. She looked a whole lot like Mom, her twin, when she did that. Was she as smart as Mom at figuring out when Emma was telling a lie?

"Emma," she said slowly, "you *are* a rascal. Okay, I won't turn on the light. But you have to call me the minute you get home."

"Okay, okay, I will," Emma said. "But Auntie Liz—don't tell Mom, okay?"

Auntie Liz screwed up her face. "I should. But I won't. Okay, now, scoot." And she gave Emma a little pat on the bottom.

Emma ran down the hall, through the big room, and out of the house. She hopped off the porch, not even turning to say good-bye to Marmaduke.

She zoomed down the path, praying that there were no bears following her. Praying that Max would stay awake long enough to get Marmaduke into the house. Praying that he could hide Marmaduke safely in the closet. Praying like mad that Auntie Liz didn't suspect a thing.

Emma was afraid that maybe she was praying for way too much.

Chapter Ten

Just a Nightmare

When Emma got home, she quietly dialed Auntie Liz, just as she'd promised. She said that she hadn't met any bears—or moths—and that she was home safely and she was going straight to bed.

She didn't go to bed, though. Instead, she stood at the bottom of the ladder to the loft where Annie slept. A tiny light was shining up above, like a night-light. Was Annie awake, reading, maybe?

Emma stood still, holding her breath, listening. No sounds, nothing. She needed to talk to Annie, to tell her the truth. She couldn't ever keep secrets from Annie. She'd tell about the trees. And about hiding Marmaduke at Max's. Emma hadn't wanted to tell about Marmaduke until after he had been safely hidden. She had a feeling Annie might not like it too much. But Emma was pretty sure that Annie would understand *why* she'd had to do it.

Silently, in bare feet, Emma climbed up the ladder, one careful, slow step at a time. When her head popped up into the opening, she peered around.

In the far corner, where the roof sloped down, was Annie's bed. And Annie lay in it, fast asleep. The little lamp on her bedside table was lit, and a book was lying open on her tummy, where it must have dropped when she fell asleep reading.

Emma tiptoed across the loft. Carefully, she removed the book from Annie's tummy and laid it on the floor. Then, silently, she crept into bed alongside Annie.

Annie sighed. She didn't open her eyes, but she turned and slid an arm around Emma, hugging her close. "Mmm," Annie murmured.

"Mmm," Emma said back. She lay quietly, breathing in happily. She'd been worried and in trouble all day long—or she would be soon enough. For now, it was nice just to lie there and snuggle.

"You okay, me dear?" Annie whispered after a while.

"I'm okay," Emma said.

"Are your mum and daddy quite upset?" Annie asked.

"I didn't tell them yet," Emma said.

Annie opened her eyes. "You didn't? And why didn't you?"

"Because." And then Emma spilled out the whole story—about her tree and the people who were going to cut it down and everything. When she got to the part about taking Marmaduke over to Max's house, Annie sat straight up. She sat up so fast, she bumped her head on the sloping ceiling.

"Ouch!" she said.

She lay back down.

"Annie, I had to!" Emma said, reaching over and rubbing Annie's head for her. "If I left him in the car, he'd get lonely. And hot. And hungry. And your car would smell. You know his cage needs cleaning every day."

"But, me dear, what are we going to do about your mum and daddy? You *have* to tell them."

"I know!" Emma said. "As soon as I get those ribbons cut off, I will."

"They'll be upset that you've kept it secret for so long, though," Annie whispered. "Why, they may even be upset at me."

"No!" Emma whispered back. "Not at you. Because it's not like I did anything really bad. I mean, if I'd pushed someone in the lake or stolen something, then you'd have to tell. Right away. Right?"

"Right," Annie said.

"So this isn't really bad, so they won't be really mad," Emma said.

They were both quiet awhile.

After a bit, Emma said, "Annie? Sneaking Marmaduke wasn't really bad, was it? It's just . . . maybe, naughty. But Annie, it's not too naughty if you really, really *need* your pet. Is it?"

Annie hugged Emma closer. "Me dear," she whispered, "I'm sleepy. It was a long drive and a long day. I can't even think straight right now. Can we just go to sleep? Maybe when I wake up in the morning, I'll find out that this was all just a wee nightmare."

"It's not," Emma said.

"Let's go to sleep, anyway," Annie said.

"Okay," Emma said. "Can I sleep here with you?"

"But of course," Annie answered. And she turned over and within a moment, was breathing deeply and slowly.

Emma was sleepy, too. It had been a long day and a hard day for her, too. Before she fell asleep, though, she wondered—*if you did bad things, did God still answer your prayers?*

She thought maybe God did. He had to. Otherwise, kids would never get their way about anything. At least, not kids like her.

So even though she wasn't sure it would work, she said a prayer that everything would turn out just fine. And in a minute, Emma, just like Annie, was fast asleep.

Chapter Eleven
Summer Rules

Maybe God had been listening. Maybe her prayers had been answered. Because the next morning, the whole family was sitting around on the screened-in porch having breakfast, talking and laughing. Tim was stretched flat out on the floor reading a book, and the little kids were running in and out. McClain was chasing Kelley. Woof was chasing McClain. Everything was just like normal.

Max, Uncle Max, and Auntie Liz were there, too. They had come over early, and Auntie Liz hadn't even frowned at Emma. She just kissed Emma good morning and hugged her close, as though she hadn't caught Emma sneaking around in the middle of the night, pretending to be deathly scared of moths.

Emma had already pulled Max aside and found out the one thing that really mattered—that

Marmaduke was safely hidden. Not only that, Max had snuggled with Marmaduke in bed for a while. That made Emma so happy, knowing Marmaduke had been loved.

The only not-so-good thing was Annie. When they'd woken up, Annie had looked very worried, but she hadn't scolded—Annie never scolded. She did say, though, that she thought Emma was getting herself in "deeper and deeper." But Annie also seemed really upset about Emma's tree and all those trees being cut down.

"Indeed, it's a shame," Annie said, shaking her head. "Imagine cutting down those beautiful old trees, and just for the likes of a better view."

For a moment, Emma even thought that maybe Annie was going to offer to help. But all Annie had said was, "I think, me dear, that I saw some good, strong scissors in the drawer by the kitchen sink."

Now they had all finished breakfast and were planning their day. Mom and Auntie Liz were going to sit and chat over coffee for a while. Daddy and Tim and Uncle Max were going fishing. McClain said she'd go, too—if she finished her project. She was cutting a hole in a shoebox, making a trap for catching chipmunks. Annie had already buckled the twins into their life vests and had led them down to the lake for a swimming lesson. And Emma was heading off to the woods with Max.

Except—Daddy called a halt. "Hang on, gang!" he said. "We have to go over the rules first. The summer rules. You ran off yesterday before we had a chance to remind you."

"Daddy!" Emma said, flopping back down into a rocking chair. "We know the rules. We've heard them a zillion times."

"Two zillion!" Tim said. He didn't even look up from his book.

"I could do them in my sleep!" Max said.

"Okay, then," Daddy said. "Go ahead, let's hear."

Emma rolled her eyes. "Always wear a life jacket when you go out in the boat."

"Listen for the gong," Max said. "Come home when it sounds."

"Watch out for the little kids, especially when they're on the dock," Tim said, still not looking up from his book. "That's what big brothers do."

"And sisters," Emma said.

"And cousins," Max said.

"Never swim alone!" Emma said. She raised her eyebrows and smiled at Daddy.

Daddy grinned back.

"Respect the environment," Tim said.

"He means, don't litter," Max said.

"Don't pick blueberries on other people's property unless the people say you can," Emma said. "Don't—"

"Don't chase bears!" McClain piped up.

"What?" Mom said.

"Bears!" McClain said. "You should stay away from bears."

Daddy nodded. "Well, yes. That is a good rule."

"But you can chase chipmunks," McClain said.

"Okay, okay!" Daddy said, laughing. "I guess you guys know the rules."

"One more thing," Uncle Max added, "and this is important: Stay away from the Thompsons' house. There's all sorts of construction equipment moving in." He turned to Daddy. "I saw Tom Thompson this morning when I went into town for the paper."

Daddy made a face and shook his head. "More loads of gravel and concrete?"

Uncle Max nodded. "Yeah, a monster cement mixer. And those huge cherry-picker things for cutting down trees."

Emma sucked in her breath. She didn't dare look at Max.

Auntie Liz turned to Mom. "Can you believe what

those . . . those . . . people are doing?" She said _people_ like it was a dirty word. "That beautiful prope.., isn't going to have a single tree left!"

Oh, yes it is, thought Emma.

"I know," Mom said. "It's hard to imagine what kind of people would do a thing like that. They are just—impossible! Destroying trees just for a 'view'?"

McClain looked up from the chipmunk trap. "I know what _impossible_ means," she said. "It means they're bad, right?"

Mom laughed. "Not really, sweetie. I'm sure they're not bad, and I probably shouldn't have said that. It's just that I'm really upset with the whole situation."

"_Actually_," McClain said, using one of her favorite words, "I'm upset, too."

"Daddy? Mom?" Emma said. "Can we go now?"

Daddy nodded. "I think so."

"Wait!" Auntie Liz said. "One more rule. You forgot."

Don't go running around in the middle of the night. Emma sent a look to Auntie Liz. _You promised not to tell._

"Have fun!" Auntie Liz said, smiling. "That's the most important rule. It's what summer's all about. Go and enjoy!"

Emma jumped up. So did Max. They took off.

Forget 'enjoy,' Emma thought. There was important stuff to do. And it had to be done quickly, before the cherry pickers started their dirty work.

Chapter Twelve

Up in the Tree

Together, Emma and Max ran along the deer path. Emma had sneaked off with the kitchen scissors and Max had his Swiss Army knife.

Emma heard the machines before she saw them—a low rumble, a muttering kind of sound. The closer they got to the Thompsons' house, the louder the sound.

The sun was up now, glittering off the trees, the wind shifting the leaves so that the sun and shade made a kind of patchwork quilt all around them. It was beautiful. Emma knew it was beautiful. She didn't stop to look, but she knew it inside her heart.

When they got to the fork in the path, the place where the two paths diverged, they stopped.

Emma's tree.

Still there. Still safe. But still wrapped up in that

awful, yellow ribbon. Emma could hear the machines coming closer. They hadn't come to claim her tree, though. Not yet. Not ever.

She rested her head against the tree trunk. This time, she didn't care if Max saw.

"I'm here," she whispered. "Don't be afraid. They're not going to cut you down." She stayed that way for a minute, just leaning her forehead against the tree.

"Emma?" Max said.

"What?"

"What are you doing?"

Emma turned to him. "Talking to my tree!" she said. "Okay?"

"Oh!" Max said. He shrugged. "Okay. Whatever."

"Okay." Emma took the big kitchen scissors and slid the point between the trunk of the tree and the yellow ribbon. Only it wasn't a ribbon after all—it was a plastic tape and it was tough. It didn't cut easily.

She snipped—but the scissors didn't cut through. She fiddled with the scissors and tried again. Nothing.

"These scissors stink!" she said.

"Let me try," Max said. "Come on. My knife is sharp. Move over."

"Okay, okay," Emma said. "Don't be so bossy." She moved back to make room for Max. He slid

71

the blade of his knife under the tape. It took just a minute, a few sawing motions, and the tape began to fray.

"There!" he said. "Got it."

And he did. The yellow tape fluttered to the ground and lay at their feet.

"Yippee!" Emma said, and she smiled. Safe. Her tree was safe. She bent and picked up the tape. Where to put it? She didn't have any pockets in her shorts. Besides, the tape was long and thick and bulky. Also dirty. She looked around for a place to hide it.

Max was patting his pockets. "No more room," he said.

"Bury it?" Emma said.

Max nodded. He frowned. "Should we rescue other trees, too?"

"No!" Emma said. "I mean, yes. I mean, I don't know."

"How come?" Max said. "I mean, how come you don't know?"

"I don't know why I don't know," Emma said.

How could she explain? This was her woods. It belonged to her. All winter she had thought about this wood, these trees, the deer path, *her* tree. It was hers. It belonged to her. Except it didn't, really. It didn't belong to her at all, except in her heart.

Someone else had bought a big part of it. And they were destroying it. Killing her trees. There wouldn't even be places for the deer to hide.

Still, wouldn't it be wrong to cut the tapes? And would it really make any difference? Wouldn't someone just put the tapes back on?

"We saved *this* tree," Max said.

"I know," Emma said. "This one's different, though. Special."

"I have an idea," Max said.

"What?" Emma said.

"We could cut the tape off the big trees," Max said, "and tie it on the little ones. It doesn't matter as much if they cut down the small ones."

"You think so?" Emma said. "Maybe. I guess. Because the old ones are bigger and give more shade. And more places for the deer to hide."

"And," Max said, "more acorns for the deer and—"

"And Mr. Thompson won't notice so much," Emma said. "Come on. Let's climb. I can think better up in the tree."

She dropped the yellow tape on the ground, then reached above and hooked her arm over the lowest branch. She pulled herself up, Max right behind.

It took only a moment or two before they got to

Emma's favorite spot. It was high up where the tree split, as if it were trying to become two trees. One part leaned out toward the lake; the other stretched back toward the wood. There were two broad, flat branches, right where the tree forked.

Emma settled herself on one, Max on the other.

Emma sighed happily and looked around her. If it weren't for the rumble of the machines off in the distance, she would have been perfectly happy. Her place. Her tree. Even her birds. She could hear a cardinal. *Purdy, purdy, purdy*, he called. Emma smiled.

"Hear that, Max?" she said. "That's a cardinal, a boy cardinal."

"How do you know it's a boy?" Max asked.

"I just do," Emma said. But then she wondered if she was right. Where had she learned that? There were so many things that she knew, but she didn't know how she knew them.

Emma peered through the leaves. She could barely make out the lake. She could make out rowboats, people fishing maybe, the boats just small black dots. A tiny silver sliver of something— a sailboat—moved way out on the lake. There was a motion on the path below, and Emma looked down.

A deer—three deer—a mother and two fawns.

74

They had stopped almost at the base of the tree and were nibbling on some ferns. The yellow tape that Emma had dropped was right at the feet of one of the fawns. She shouldn't have dropped it there! She hoped the fawn wouldn't get tangled in it.

Emma motioned Max to look down, too. They watched as all three deer nibbled, darting, stepping this way and that. At one point, the big doe raised her head and looked up into the branches. A bunch of leaves was sticking out of her mouth as she chewed.

Emma kept super-still. After a minute, the doe bent her head and went back to her breakfast. Emma could hear the rumble of the machines, louder now. Were they moving closer?

The big doe seemed to hear, also. She lifted her head again. She held it high for a long time, her nostrils moving in and out. Her ears perked up. Her white tail began to swish, flickering back and forth. And then, she must have given a silent signal, because she leaped for the underbrush, followed immediately by her fawns.

They disappeared so thoroughly, there was no sign they had ever been by the tree at all. But the yellow tape was still there. Lying in plain view.

Something else was coming into view. A pickup

truck. Behind it was a huge, blue truck. The blue truck had a gigantic, metal rod on top with a cage attached. Emma recognized it as the machine Uncle Max had called a cherry picker, the machine that cut down trees. It made a dreadful noise, creeping toward them through the trees, crunching branches and small shrubs underneath like a dinosaur on wheels.

"I need to get that ribbon, that tape!" Emma whispered. "They'll see it!"

"You can't!" Max said. "They're too close. They'll see you."

"No," Emma said. "I'm quick. I can do it. Wait and see."

"Emma, no!" Max said.

But Emma was already on her way.

Chapter Thirteen

Emma to the Rescue

Emma clambered down from her perch, reaching for footholds, handholds, down, down, down, like a squirrel or a chipmunk. When she thought she was low enough, she peeked out from the branches. The truck was closing in. But not close enough that anyone in the truck could see her. She hoped. There was a dog in the back of the pickup, a small, brown dog. She leaped the last few feet to the ground.

Ouch! She twisted her ankle a little, but still, she bent, snatched up the yellow tape, stuffed it inside her shirt, and scurried back up the tree.

Behind her, Emma could hear the trucks rumbling closer. She turned and peered through the leaves again. They were so close now that she could see the faces of the men in the pickup. She could also see the dog better—small and fat, with a white patch around one eye.

Had they seen her? No. She didn't think so. They'd been awfully close, though.

Emma turned back and scampered higher and higher. She reached the branch across from Max, her heart racing madly.

"They didn't see me," she whispered.

"I could see them," Max whispered back. "Real easy."

"It's okay, it's okay," Emma said. "I'm sure they didn't see me."

She wasn't sure. But she hoped.

The pickup truck stopped, almost directly beneath their tree, but the monster blue truck kept creeping toward the lake. A man in a hard hat climbed out of the pickup. He stood beside it, looking around.

Emma willed herself to become perfectly still. Beside her, Max was holding his breath. They were both clutching their branches tightly, as still as if they were dead.

Hard Hat walked away from the pickup. He looked at the tree. He circled it. He walked a few steps one way, then a few the other way. He came back and stopped right beneath them. He looked up.

Emma closed her eyes. She tried to make herself invisible.

The dog in the truck began to bark, a high, yippy sound, much too high and yippy for a fat dog.

"Hush, Poochie," the man said.

Emma opened her eyes. *Poochie?* Again, she looked down. The man had taken off his helmet. He wiped his head with a handkerchief. From up above, Emma could see that he was very, very bald. For some reason, it made her want to giggle. She imagined herself dropping an acorn on his big, bald head.

He put his hard hat back on and called to someone inside the truck. "Hal! Didn't we mark this tree?" he yelled. "I remember marking one at the fork of this path. This is the one that blocks the view from the porch, isn't it?"

The man in the truck answered, but Emma couldn't hear what he said.

"Weird," Hard Hat said. He looked down at a paper in his hand. He scratched his neck. "I'll have to check the master list. Well, I'm paying that tree guy by the hour, so let's go catch up. We got ten trees to do before this day is over."

Ten trees? He was going to cut down *ten* trees. All today? And how many after that?

Hard Hat got back into the truck. After a moment, the pickup drove off, following the big blue truck toward the lake.

When they were gone, Emma turned to Max. "Okay," she said. "They're going to the lake; we're going up the hill."

She scooted down from the tree, reaching with her feet from branch to branch, till she got to the bottom. Max followed right behind.

"'Bye, tree!" she said, once she landed on the ground, wincing a bit from her painful ankle. "We'll be back later. Don't worry. You're safe."

They raced along the path, away from the lake and up the hill toward the Thompsons' house. Where there were bunches of doomed trees circled with plastic ribbons. Just waiting to be rescued.

Chapter Fourteen

Mr. Thompson Comes to Call

By lunchtime, Emma was pooped. She and Max had cut lots of tapes off lots of trees. They hadn't saved every single tree—they knew that if there were no yellow ribbons left on any trees, it would be too suspicious—but they had saved a bunch of the bigger trees. They had also tied tapes to some of the smaller trees as Max had suggested. For some reason, that made Emma feel a little guilty, as though she were condemning a baby tree to death. Still, little trees sprang up easily all over the place. Emma decided that she and Max could plant some acorns in a day or two. That way, the acorns would grow into some huge oak trees to replace the ones that would be cut down.

They had also dug out a soft spot under some bushes—using their hands since they hadn't brought along a shovel—and buried the telltale yellow tapes in a shallow kind of grave. When they were finished, they rolled a rotted log on top to be sure the tapes would stay hidden. It had been hard, hot work.

Emma felt happy. Her tree was safe. And even though she felt a teeny bit guilty about what she had done, it was over.

Max went to his house to have lunch and get his bathing suit, and Emma went home, too. She wanted to take a swim and cool off. And once she had done that . . . she sighed . . . it would be time to tell about Marmaduke. Well, at least she could stop feeling guilty about that.

Emma was a little scared, though. Mom and Daddy would be awfully mad. So when to tell? Right now? Get it over with, as Annie had said? Or wait? Maybe she should tell at dinnertime. Dinner was always a madhouse. Mom and Daddy were so busy at dinner—cutting up food for the little kids, pouring milk, and everything—that they wouldn't have time to get mad.

Yeah, dinnertime would be good.

Oh, rats! Emma stopped dead in her tracks. Mom and Daddy would want to know where Marmaduke was. Then Max would be in trouble, too.

Suddenly, a brilliant thought popped into Emma's head. She saw Max every day during the summer.

She was always at his house or he at hers. Marmaduke could live with Max all summer, and she could go see Marmaduke every day and play with him and cuddle him. It would be almost the same as having him at the lake house. Then, at the end of the summer, she could sneak him back home in Annie's car, just the way she had gotten him here. That way, she'd never have to tell. Nobody would know. And nobody would get into trouble. Not Annie. Not Max. Not Emma.

Perfect.

But then she thought, *No, Annie wouldn't agree to that plan.*

Oh, boy. Annie had been right—putting things off just made everything harder. Well, she'd just think about it some more while she swam.

When she got back to the house, she found the whole family gathered on the screened-in porch. Auntie Liz and Uncle Max had gone home, but everyone else was there.

Mom and Daddy were sitting side by side on one of the two big swings, drinking coffee and reading the newspaper. Ira was on the floor with Lizzie, the two of them pushing around a pile of pebbles and making a road. Annie was helping them. Tim was on the floor, too, reading with his head on Woof as if Woof were just a pillow. And McClain was on the other big swing, rocking and hugging Kelley up under her chin.

"Emma, Emma!" McClain yelled as soon as Emma came up on the porch. "Guess what? Guess what? I caught a fish! All by myself. Tim got one, and I got one. But mine was bigger."

"Show Emma how big your fish was," Tim said.

Emma sat down beside McClain and pulled her up onto her lap. McClain snuggled into Emma, dumping Kelley onto the floor.

"How big?" Emma asked.

"Big!" McClain said. She held up her little pudgy hand. "As big as my hand. What kind of fish was it, Daddy? I forget."

"A bass," Daddy said.

"That's not nice!" Ira said, looking up from his road.

"It's a swearword," Lizzie said.

Daddy laughed. "No, it's not," he said. "I said, bass. Buh . . . buh . . . bass."

"Am I allowed to say that word?" Ira asked.

Daddy nodded.

"Bass, bass, bass," Ira said.

He and Lizzie burst into giggles.

"McClain was a real fisherman," Daddy said, smiling at the twins. "She even put the bait on all by herself."

"It was a worm," McClain said. "I cut it in half and got two worms. Both sides wiggled."

"Weird!" Emma said.

"What did you do all morning, Emma?" Daddy asked.

Emma shrugged. She buried her face in McClain's curls. "Just played around. Climbed trees with Max. And stuff."

She didn't dare look at Annie.

"Listen!" Mom said suddenly, looking up from her newspaper. "Hear that sound? That splash?"

They all stopped talking and listened. The sound came again.

"That's a fish jumping out in the lake," Mom said. "That's how quiet it is here. When that impossible man doesn't have his machines going. Like they were all morning. Auntie Liz and I could barely hear one another out here on the porch. We finally went inside to talk."

Daddy nodded. "I know. It's a wonder we caught even one fish with all that racket," he said.

"I hear bees," McClain said. "Lots of them."

"I think you're hearing a motorboat," Daddy said.

And sure enough, in a minute, a small boat came into view. McClain had been right, Emma thought. It did sound like a bunch of really loud bees. It puttered right up to the little dock at the foot of the path to their house and stopped.

A man in the boat stood up and waved. He threw out a rope, jumped onto the dock, and began tying up the boat. A little dog was in the back of his boat. A fat brown dog. With a white patch around one eye.

Daddy turned to Mom. "I wonder . . . is that Mr. Thompson? Looks like him."

It was! Emma was sure of it. The man who'd been chopping down trees. He wasn't wearing his hard hat. His bald head was shining in the sun. What was he here for? Had he recognized Emma, seen her in the woods? Had he come to tell on her? Her heart began thundering away like crazy.

"I don't know," Mom said. "It might be the lobster man from the fish store. He said he'd deliver the lobsters."

No. It wasn't the lobster man. It was Mr. Thompson.

"Yobsters?" Ira said.

"L-l-l-obsters," Daddy said, drawing out the *L* sound for Ira.

"Claws!" Lizzie said.

"Yet's go see!" Ira said.

"Wait!" Annie said.

86

Daddy and Annie both jumped up. But the twins had already gotten to their feet, flung open the screen door, and were racing down toward the dock. They were going so fast that Lizzie tumbled and fell, but she quickly picked herself up and ran on.

And then, before either Annie or Daddy could get out the door, the little ones were charging at the bald man at the dock. He scooped them up into his arms.

Daddy hustled out the door and down the path. There was a big commotion, with the dog in the boat yipping away, Daddy scolding the twins and shaking hands with the man, and Ira yelling about where were the yobsters. Within about a minute, the whole bunch of them—except for the little dog that was on a leash tied to the boat—was coming back up the path. Daddy was carrying Lizzie, and the man still had Ira in his arms.

When they came up onto the porch, the twins jumped down and went back to their roadwork again, and Annie joined them.

"Everybody," Daddy said, "meet our new neighbor. This is Mr. Thompson. He's bought that house and property down the lake a ways."

"Tommy," the man said. "Tommy Thompson."

Well, if that wasn't the stupidest name ever!

"Tommy," Daddy said, "meet my family." Daddy went through all the names, including Kelley and Woof.

Everyone said hi and hello—well, the humans did, anyway—and Mom stood up and shook Mr. Thompson's hand and so did Annie and Tim, and then they all sat back down. Emma didn't get up. She just said hi and kept herself kind of hidden behind McClain's curls.

"Thanks for catching those little ones," Daddy said. "You moved fast. Can we get you a cup of coffee or something? Something cold, maybe?"

Mr. Thompson shook his head. "Nope, have work to do. But the wife asked me to come and tell you that we'd like you all to join us for a picnic. Can't invite you to the house yet since it's not near to finished. But we'll do a picnic outside on Thursday, a barbecue. We'd like to get to know our neighbors."

"That's very sweet of you," Mom said.

"Bring the gang," Mr. Thompson said, waving his hand around. "Kids—everybody! We'll have all the ribs you can eat. And some real Southern barbecue. We thought we'd bring a bit of the South up here to Maine. How's that sound?"

"Well," Mom said, "it sounds lovely." She sent a look to Daddy. "I think we'd like that, wouldn't we?"

Daddy nodded. "We would. Thank you very much."

"Then I'll tell the wife you said yes," Mr. Thompson said. "She'll be real tickled."

"Tickled? Why?" McClain asked.

Mr. Thompson laughed. "I meant that she'll be real happy."

"You're impossible!" McClain said.

"McClain!" Mom said. "Mind your manners."

Mr. Thompson laughed again. "Impossible? My wife thinks so, too, sometimes."

"So does Mom," McClain said.

"McClain!" Mom said again. She patted her lap. "Come over here."

McClain didn't move. Instead, she turned and buried her face in Emma's shoulder. Emma knew McClain felt embarrassed. But she'd only said out loud what everyone else had said. And thought.

Mr. Thompson burst out laughing again. It seemed he laughed a lot. Mom and Daddy weren't laughing, though. They looked weird. Mom's ears had turned red.

Still, McClain was right. Mr. Thompson *was* impossible. Cutting down ten trees in one day! Emma didn't want to go to his picnic at all. There was no way she'd eat anything he cooked. For all she knew, he could be cooking deer!

"I'll be going, then," Mr. Thompson said. He stood up. He shook hands with Daddy. He said good-bye to Mom. He turned to go.

But then, at the door to the porch, he turned back. "I hear local folks have been calling our place the haunted house," he said.

"Oh, that's just nonsense," Daddy said.

"It's because nobody's lived there for a long time," Tim said. "In books, they always call old, empty houses haunted houses."

Mr. Thompson nodded. "I guess. It's mighty strange, though. Things do seem to move around on the property. Get lost. Misplaced. Disappear. It worries the wife quite a bit. Bothers me, too."

He was looking right at Emma when he said that. He raised his eyebrows, as if he were asking her a question. Then he shook his head, turned, and left.

Emma thought: *He knows! He knows!*

What a dilemma!

So what? Even if he did, he couldn't prove a thing.

She hoped.

Chapter Fifteen
Lucky Emma

The birds awakened Emma. She looked at her Mickey Mouse watch. Four thirty, not yet light, just faint daylight creeping through the curtains. But the birds were saying it was morning. They were twittering like crazy. It seemed the whole world was alive with birds.

Emma sat up. She hadn't told about Marmaduke last night. But she would tell today. Definitely today. First, though, she'd spend her morning in her tree. When she was in Maine, this was her very favorite time of day. She pushed back her quilt and got out of bed, shivering a little in the cold air. Quickly, she pulled on a T-shirt and shorts, then her sweatshirt, the yellow and black one from her soccer team, the Hornets. She picked up the book she'd been reading last night, *Anne of Green Gables*, and tiptoed out to the kitchen.

As soon as Woof saw her up and about, he came begging to be let out. Emma patted him. "Not now," she whispered. "You'll chase the deer away."

In the kitchen, she made herself a peanut butter sandwich on mushy white bread, the only kind of bread that was just right with peanut butter. She looked around for a banana but didn't see one. Peanut butter and banana was the best sandwich in the world. But plain peanut butter was second best.

There were a couple of apples and peaches in the fruit bowl on the table. Emma took one peach, two apples, and her sandwich. She dropped them into one of the recycle string bags Mom kept in the kitchen. Then she went to the fridge and got a bottle of apple juice and dropped that in, too. She also put in *Anne of Green Gables* and started for the door. But then she remembered. She had to leave a note. Though she was allowed to go just about anywhere here at the lake, she always had to let Mom and Daddy know where. She scribbled a fast note: *In my tree!*

She hesitated just a minute, then got another piece of paper. She wrote *Annie: Today. Promis.*

She knew Annie would understand what she meant. Emma hadn't told last night because the twins had been sick and throwing up. First one threw up, then the other, then the first one again.

It had gotten kind of crazed. Emma had thought it wasn't the best time to tell about Marmaduke. Annie had agreed. Especially when McClain had started throwing up, too.

Emma set the notes on the table and tiptoed to the door. Woof nosed at her knee. "Later, Woof," she whispered to him. "Maybe you can come to the coast with us when we go later."

Once outside, she started down the deer path. She hadn't been up in her tree alone since they'd arrived at the lake house. Yesterday with Max didn't count.

It was still dark, but light enough for her to see her way without a flashlight. Very quietly, she walked along, thinking. In school, she had studied about the Native American tribes. She knew that the Abenaki had lived here in Maine a long time ago, and some still did. She pretended to be an Abenaki. She tried not to make a sound, her footsteps nothing more than a whisper on the grass.

Everywhere she looked, the woods were coming alive. Not just birds but rabbits and chipmunks and squirrels were everywhere. The rabbits, big ones and little ones, scurried about in the grass. They seemed totally unafraid of her, as if they knew she would never hurt them. One bunny came so close that Emma could see his little nose twitching, his ears transparent with the light coming through them. She stopped to watch. He was right by her feet. She could have touched him if she'd wanted, but she knew that would frighten him. The bunny kept bending his head, nibbling on some grass, then looking up at her. Emma thought maybe he was asking if she wanted some, too.

"No thanks," she whispered. "I have my peanut butter."

Soon her bunny was chased by another bunny, and they both went hopping along and out of sight.

Emma walked on, thinking of her Beatrix Potter books, with the stories of Peter Rabbit and all the mischief that he got into. She thought she might like to be a bunny, just for a little while, maybe for half a day. Or else a deer. Deer were so beautiful. It seemed wondrous the way they could leap over things, almost as if they were flying. She didn't think she'd like being an owl, though. Owls ate bunnies.

And then she had a thought—maybe it wouldn't be so much fun to be a bunny after all. You couldn't run through the woods without being scared.

She reached her tree. She took out the two apples she had put into her bag and dropped them on the ground, knowing they'd attract some deer. Then she shifted her string bag so it was hanging from her arm, pushed it up around her elbow, and began to climb. She knew this tree so well, she could have climbed it with closed eyes. She knew just which branches would hold her safely, which ones were too tender to take her weight, where to reach for the next branch.

It took just moments to reach her very own place, the broad, flat branch high, high up in the tree.

Emma sighed happily as she looked around her. Then she settled herself comfortably and leaned back against the trunk. It still wasn't quite light, but from up here, she could look over the woods, the lake, all the way to the other side. She closed her eyes briefly, feeling the trees, the air, the silence.

With her eyes closed, she realized the woods weren't silent at all. They were alive with sounds—rustling, chirping, sighing, the wind moving the leaves. With her eyes still closed, she tried to identify the birds.

She heard the cardinal. He was easy—*purdy, purdy, purdy*, he called. She thought of what Max had asked her—how she knew it was a boy cardinal. She didn't know how she knew. She just knew.

Another bird called. That one she knew, too. He was a favorite, a chickadee, a black-capped chickadee, the Maine state bird. He said, *fee-bee, fee-bee, fee-bee.* Sometimes, though, he added one more note. It seemed that he was saying— *Hey, sweet-ie, hey, sweet-ie*—just to Emma.

She opened her eyes. The sun was peeking above the horizon, sending rays of light through the trees. In the distance, the lake shimmered, the water pink-and-rose colored.

Emma suddenly had a funny feeling inside— happy, but maybe even more than happy. She'd had that feeling before, always when she was outside, maybe in a tree, or walking with Daddy in the dark, or lying on her back on the dock, watching star showers. She felt so happy that she was even a little bit sad, as if the happiness was almost too big to fit inside her.

The chickadee called to her again. Hey, sweet-ie! Hey, sweet-ie!"

"Hey, sweetie, yourself!" Emma called back softly.

She took out her peanut butter sandwich, opened her book, and settled back again against the trunk. She loved *Anne of Green Gables*. Anne loved trees, too. Anne had her very own apple tree, with fluffy white flowers right outside her bedroom window. Emma wished she had a tree like that outside her bedroom window. But she had this tree.

Lucky Anne.

Lucky Emma.

Chapter Sixteen
Stop!

Emma's bottom was getting numb. She shifted around on her branch, trying to make herself more comfortable. The sun was higher now, and soon it would be time to go back home. The family had planned to drive to the coast for the day to see the lighthouses and the rocky ocean front. Every summer they took a trip to the coastal town where a famous artist had painted pictures, and Emma loved it. The ocean was beautiful, but beautiful in a different way from the lakes.

Here, the lake sat calm and quiet, day and night, always the same. But the ocean was wild, roaring and beating itself against the rocks, throwing up huge white sprays into the air. There was one spot called Thunder Hole, where the waves rushed into a hole in the rocks, then rushed out again, making a crashing sound like thunder. Emma thought it would be great fun to swim in that wild kind of water.

There were also seagulls all around the coast, and they were wild, too. Sometimes, Emma and Tim and McClain would hold up bread, and the seagulls would come swooping down to snatch it right out of their hands. Both Emma and Tim ducked when the seagulls swooped in, even though they kept their hands up high holding the bread. But not McClain. She stood straight and tall and didn't duck at all. McClain wasn't scared of anything.

Of course, the twins had been too little to join the older kids and the seagulls. But that had been last year. Maybe this year, they'd want to hold up bread, too. If their tummy aches were gone. And then Emma thought of Annie. Annie had never been to Maine before. It would be great fun to see if Annie was brave with the seagulls. Emma kind of thought Annie would be.

Emma began packing up her breakfast, putting the half sandwich she hadn't eaten, the juice bottle, and the peach pit inside the string bag. She never left litter in the forest.

She looked down. Odd that the deer hadn't come this morning to eat her apples. They almost always did. She'd just leave the apples, anyway, and the deer could have them after she'd gone.

Emma wondered if they'd know the apples were a present from her.

Off in the distance, she heard a sound—the mutter of engines, the cherry picker just revving up. Is that why the deer hadn't come? They had extra-sensitive ears. They had probably heard the noise long before Emma had.

It made Emma mad. But she wasn't going to let it spoil her wonderful morning. Besides, she and Max had rescued a bunch of the trees. And this tree. *Her* tree.

She stood on her branch to take one last look around. She stretched to look out over the forest toward the lake. Funny. Now that the sun was high, she realized she could see the lake clearly. Usually, from here, the lake was mostly hidden by leaves and trees, with just a glimmer of water shining through. And then she realized—there were no trees, no trees at all. Ahead of her, between the deer path and the lake, almost every single tree was gone—sheared off at the top or gone completely. Gone! Gone!

The cherry picker was getting closer now, moving through the woods toward her. Emma could hear it, and feel it, too.

Her tree trembled a bit, as if afraid. "It's all right," Emma whispered, patting the tree trunk.

"You're safe."

In a moment, the trucks came into view—two trucks, the pickup she had seen yesterday, and the cherry picker. The pickup pulled up close beside her tree. And stopped. Right there, right beside her tree! The same brown dog sat in back. Two men climbed out. One was a fat man in an orange shirt. The other was Mr. Thompson. Hard hat and all, she recognized him. He turned toward the cherry picker and waved at the flattened path that had been made by the cherry picker yesterday.

"Come on, come on!" he yelled. "Roll forward. It's clear. It's clear. Come on, come ahead."

"Slow, slow, come slow!" Orange Shirt yelled. "Don't want you tipping over."

"Stop!" Emma yelled down. "Stop!"

But the men couldn't hear her. The truck engine, the gravel crunching, it was all too loud. But then it got quieter as the cherry picker rolled to a stop, right alongside the pickup.

"Okay!" Mr. Thompson yelled out. "Okay. We're set. Swing the boom this way."

Her tree! They were going to cut down *her* tree!

"Stop!" Emma yelled. "Stop! You can't!"

Mr. Thompson held up one hand, as if to stop the cherry picker. He turned and looked around. "What?" he yelled. "Who said that?"

"Me!" Emma yelled. "Stop! You can't cut down this tree!"

"Who is that?" he said. He peered up into the tree. "Is somebody up there? Who's up there? What are you doing up there?"

Emma didn't answer.

"Looks to me like you got a girl in your tree," Orange Shirt said. "Or maybe a boy."

"What are you doing up there?" Mr. Thompson called up again. "Are you the kid I met yesterday? Are you Tim?"

"No!" Emma said. "I'm me, Emma. And, yes, you met me yesterday. You're not cutting down this tree."

Her heart was in her throat, and she was scared and angry and crazed, and she knew she was going to be in big trouble. Bigger trouble than she'd ever been in before. But she was not going to let them cut down her tree.

"Emma, is it? Was that your name? Well, come down from there, lil' lady," Mr. Thompson said softly. "Come on, come down right now."

"No!" Emma said.

"Emma!" Mr. Thompson said. "Come on, honey." She could hear the tone of his voice. He was trying to be reasonable. Like she was just a dumb little kid. "Come on. Let's talk about it."

"No," she said.

She watched Mr. Thompson and Orange Shirt put their heads together. The driver of the cherry picker got out and came over and joined them. They all peered up into the tree.

"Emma!" Mr. Thompson said. "Come down, and we'll pretend this never happened."

Emma didn't answer.

The fat dog began to make yippy sounds, very loud and yippy, as if he were getting into the act, too.

The men spoke together again.

"Emma," Mr. Thompson called up, "I'm mighty close to going to get your papa."

"Or the police," Orange Shirt yelled up.

Emma still didn't answer. What was there left to say? Nothing. She sat down on the branch. What could they do? What could she do? They wouldn't cut the tree down with her in it. Would they? No, they wouldn't. She could get hurt. Killed.

She didn't care. She was not moving from this tree. She still had half her peanut butter sandwich. Most of her apple juice. She had her book. She could stay here a very, very long time.

Forever even.

Chapter Seventeen
Good-bye, Tree

All became quiet down below. Mr. Thompson and Orange Shirt and the cherry picker guy piled into the little pickup truck and sped off. Emma was pretty sure she knew where they were going—to tell on her, to find Daddy and tell him. And what would Daddy do? Would he be mad? He'd definitely tell her to come down.

So what? She wouldn't.

For a long time, Emma sat there, waiting, waiting, listening to the birds, listening for the sound of the truck returning, listening to her own heart beating fast and hard. Once, off in the distance, she thought she heard Daddy's voice, maybe talking to Mr. Thompson, but she couldn't be sure. Could Daddy talk Mr. Thompson out of cutting down the tree? Would he?

Probably not. And then, even though she had

promised herself that she wouldn't cry, she couldn't help it. The tears began to well up. Her tree would be gone. She knew it would be. She couldn't stop the tree cutters. She was just a kid.

After a bit, she heard the men returning, the trucks rumbling through the woods, voices, men's voices. And then . . . Daddy was there, too. Daddy!

He didn't call up to her. He didn't scold. He didn't say, "Come on down."

He climbed right up into her tree. Emma didn't even know that he knew how to climb a tree. But he did. He climbed up and settled right there beside her on her very own branch. He wrapped his arm around her. He didn't say a word. He just sat there. For a long time.

Only once did he speak, and that was to call down to the men who were circling the tree below, the truck still there, too, muttering away.

Mr. Thompson yelled, "I'm paying these tree guys by the hour. You better come down from that tree, both of you. And soon, too!"

Daddy called back, "Tell me what it costs. I'll write you a check later."

Then Daddy turned back to Emma, still hugging her close, even rocking her, not seeming to care that the branch waved and sank under them a little.

Forever, it seemed, they sat that way. Neither of

them saying a word.

Finally, Emma said, "I hate him, Daddy."

"I know," Daddy answered.

"I hate him forever and ever. And even more."

"I know," Daddy said. He didn't even scold her for saying the word *hate*.

"I *love* this tree!" Emma said.

"I know," Daddy said. "I know you do."

"It's *my* tree!" she said. "It's been my tree forever. I dream about it all winter long."

"I know," Daddy said.

"It's not *his* tree," Emma said.

"I know," Daddy said. "But it kind of is. He owns the property."

"You can't *own* a tree!" Emma said. "Only God owns trees."

"God and you?" Daddy said, smiling.

Emma didn't answer.

"If it was my very own tree," Emma said, "then nobody could cut it down. Not *ever*."

"There're plenty of trees on our property," Daddy said.

"I know. But they're not *this* tree. Anne has her own tree with white fluffy flowers right outside her bedroom window."

"Annie does?"

"No, not Annie, *Anne*."

"Who's Anne?" Daddy asked.

"Oh, just somebody," Emma said. "In a book. I keep thinking about it. I keep thinking about . . . trees."

"Oh."

"Daddy?" Emma said after a while. "Know what?"

"What?"

"I did something bad," Emma said.

"I know," Daddy said.

"You do?"

Daddy nodded.

Which bad thing did he know about? She took a chance. "You mean about those yellow tapes? On the trees?" She didn't add about Max helping her.

"Yes. I figured you might have had something to do with it," Daddy said. "Mr. Thompson said some of his trees had been—he called it—'tampered with.' He told me before."

"I'm not sorry," Emma said.

Daddy patted Emma's leg.

For a long time more, they sat there.

"Daddy?" Emma asked. "Are you hungry?"

"I am."

"I have half a sandwich," Emma said. She held out the bag to him.

Daddy took it. He took out the half of a peanut

butter sandwich. It was kind of smushed. He broke the half in half and handed one piece to Emma. She took it. It was not only smushed, but hot.

They both ate quietly for a minute. Then they shared the rest of the apple juice.

"Daddy?" Emma said. "If we climb down, is he going to cut down the tree?"

"I'm afraid so," Daddy said.

"Can't you make him change his mind?"

Daddy sighed. "I tried. Before I climbed up here, I tried. But this tree is blocking his view of the lake from his front porch. And you can't move a tree this big."

"He could move his porch," Emma said. "Or something."

"I actually thought of that," Daddy said. "But we have no right to tell him where to build his porch, sweetie."

"So if I come down, the tree comes down?"

Daddy nodded.

Emma was quiet for a very long time. And then she said, "Daddy, I have to go to the bathroom."

"Me, too," Daddy said.

"You climb down first," Emma said.

"Okay."

Carefully, Daddy put the scraps and the apple juice bottle into the string bag. He slung the handle of the bag over his arm. Then, without looking back at Emma, he began climbing down from the tree.

Emma waited till she couldn't see the top of his head anymore. Then she laid her head against her tree.

"'Bye, tree," she whispered. She swallowed hard. "Good-bye." And then she clambered down, too, reaching blindly with her feet and hands.

Good thing she knew the tree so well. Because with her tears, she wasn't able to see a thing.

Chapter Eighteen
Nothing Is Fun Anymore

"Don't cry."

That's what McClain whispered to Emma the next night, curled up beside Emma in her bed. "Please don't cry, okay?"

"I'm not crying," Emma said.

"You're breathing," McClain whispered. She was squooshed up close to Emma, her curly head pressed against Emma's chest. She had crept into Emma's bed after the whole family had gone to sleep.

Emma hugged her a little, but didn't say anything.

"Emma?" McClain whispered again. "I said, 'You're breathing.'"

"Good thing," Emma whispered back.

"Your heart's beating, too," McClain said. "I can hear it. It goes bumpity, bumpity, bump, like that."

"Will you hush?" Emma said. "I'm trying to get

to sleep. How can I sleep with you talking all the time?"

"I can sing you a sleepy song," McClain said. "Want me to?"

"No!" Emma said.

But McClain sang, anyway. "Sleepy, sleepy, sleep-sleep!" Very loud.

"No! Now I mean it. Hush!" Emma said.

"I'm trying to make you happy," McClain whispered.

Emma hugged her close. "I know. I know."

But McClain couldn't make Emma happy. Nothing could make Emma happy. Not that night, and not the next, or the next.

No, not ever, Emma decided. Her tree was gone. She had done bad things. She still hadn't told about Marmaduke and she was missing him like crazy. Letting him live at Max's wasn't at all the same as having him right here with her. And she worried that if she told about Marmaduke now, Annie and Max would be in trouble, too. Annie had been right—putting it off had just made it worse.

Besides all that, she had lost her book, *Anne of Green Gables*. She had probably left it in the tree, and it was now chopped to pieces. Just like the tree.

And then there had been Mr. Thompson's terrible barbecue.

Mr. Thompson had invited other neighbors, including Max and Auntie Liz and Uncle Max, as well as some neighbors with toddler kids from across the lake. He had even rented a huge blow-up Moonwalk Bounce House for the kids.

As if that would make up for anything!

Everything had turned out exactly the way Emma had known it would—terrible. The kids from across the lake were whiny, and they took over the whole jumping house. They fought with one another, and one of them even bit Ira. Ira bit him back. Annie, who was almost always calm and sweet, actually hauled the little biting kid off to his mom and dumped him right in her lap.

Then, Tim and McClain went to Auntie Liz's house to get her glasses because she had forgotten them. But instead of coming right back, they'd stayed away forever—leaving Emma all alone. Alone, because Max had decided to pick that day to act like a jerk. He'd just gotten a new game for his Game Boy or Nintendo or whatever it was, and all he'd done was play with it the entire day. Meanwhile, Emma had to be polite to Mr. and Mrs. Thompson, whom she hated with her whole heart and soul.

And then, the night of the barbecue, Daddy went back to where her tree used to be, to see if maybe her book was lying there in the bushes or something. It wasn't. But Daddy said that standing there, he had tried counting the rings of the stump. He figured out that her tree had been about two hundred years old.

Two hundred years! Gone now, cut down and chopped into firewood. Just so somebody stupid could sit on their stupid porch and stupidly stare at the lake which they probably wouldn't even bother to do, anyway.

Emma wished that summer was over.

Nothing was right or fun in Maine anymore.

Chapter Nineteen

A Ferret and a Snake

It was night. Black, black night. The birds weren't even making chirruping sounds yet.

"Emma!"

Someone was calling her name. She sat up. "What?" she said.

"Wake up. Wake up!"

Tim! It was Tim. He was sitting on the side of her bed. "Get up. Get dressed, quick," Tim whispered.

"Why? What's the matter?"

"Max. He needs you. He needs us."

"Max?" she said. "Why? Is it . . . ?"

Oh, no! Marmaduke! It was Marmaduke. He'd escaped. He was always escaping. Emma had warned Max. *Don't let him out of his cage!*

"It's not Marmaduke," Tim said, as if he were reading her mind. "Don't worry. I know about Marmaduke. He's okay. But Flamester's missing."

"You know about Marmaduke? How? I mean . . . Uh oh. Flamester's missing?" Emma said.

"Yeah," Tim whispered. "Come on, I told Max we'd be there in a minute. He came looking for you. I was out on the porch, and I told him I'd wake you up and we'd both come. He ran back home. He's kind of worried."

Kind of worried? Ferrets eat snakes. If they catch them. Had Flamester made his way into Marmaduke's cage? Or had Marmaduke gotten into the aquarium cage? It was too awful to think about— her pet eating Max's pet!

Emma slid out of bed. It was freezing. She always forgot how cold it was at night in Maine. She reached around for the clothes she had dumped on the floor last night.

"Don't look!" she said to Tim.

Tim turned away.

Emma took off her jammies, then pulled on jeans and her ratty sweatshirt. She reached around for her Crocs, too, and slid her feet into them. She was glad she had a pair lined with fuzzy stuff.

"You can look now," she told Tim. "Let's go."

Together, they went quietly to the porch. As usual, Woof started to pad his way out behind them, but Emma shooed him back inside. She shut the door, feeling a little guilty about leaving him behind. He began to whine and pace around. She blew him a kiss through the screen.

Tim rooted around in the basket by the door where they kept the flashlights. He found two big ones and handed one to Emma.

Behind them, Woof was whining miserably. "Hush!" Emma whispered. "We'll be back soon."

Then, trying desperately not to make a sound, she and Tim stepped down from the porch and headed along the path, shining their lights toward their feet.

"Tim?" Emma asked. "How do you know about Marmaduke? Did Max tell you?"

"No. Well, yes," Tim answered. "But I already knew."

"You already *knew*?" Emma said it too loudly.

A crashing sound boomed from the woods behind them. Tim stepped backward and almost fell over Emma's feet. "Bears!" he whispered. He reached for Emma's hand. Emma held his tightly.

"No bears," Emma whispered. "No bears, no bears, no bears. Honest."

Or were there? The sound was coming closer.

And then, a huge deer—a buck with enormous antlers—came crashing out of the underbrush right in front of them. He leaped across the path and

116

went dashing toward the lake.

"Whew!" Emma whispered. She let go of Tim's hand. "Tim? How'd you find out about Marmaduke?"

"The day of the barbecue. When we went to Auntie Liz's house to get her glasses. Me and McClain."

"What?" Again, Emma spoke too loudly. She clapped a hand over her mouth. "McClain knows, too?"

"Yeah. She went to Max's room to get a toy. Don't worry. She won't tell."

McClain knew! McClain?

Well, Emma couldn't worry about that now. There was so much more to worry about. She was imagining herself picking up Marmaduke. She would feel along his tummy. He usually felt fat and fluffy. But would he feel lumpy if a snake were in there? If Flamester were in there? Oh, poor Max!

In a minute, they had reached Max's house. Once they were on the porch, Emma said, "Okay, turn off your flashlight."

"I won't be able to see," Tim said.

"Don't worry," Emma said. "Just hold on to my shirt."

She opened the door. She stopped. She waited till her eyes had adjusted to the dark. Silently, she made her way through the living room. Down the hall. Following the line of light coming from under Max's door.

Behind her, Tim stumbled a bit. "Ouch!" he said. He let go of her shirt.

Emma stopped. "Shhh!"

She waited. He grabbed hold of her shirt again. Then, they were at the end of the hall. They slipped inside Max's room. Emma closed the door behind them.

The bedside light was on. The room was a really awful, terrible mess. Video games and clothes and toys were tossed all over the place. Books had tumbled out of the bookcase. Everything had been dumped out of Max's desk. The closet doors were standing open. All of the bed covers were on the floor.

And there, in the midst of it all, sat Max. Winding its way around his neck and shoulders was a snake, a long, thin, brownish-gold snake. Flamester!

"You found him!" Emma said. Too loudly. She whispered, "You found him! Where?"

"Behind the books in my bookcase," Max said.

"How'd he get there?" Tim asked.

Max nodded toward the glass aquarium cage where Flamester usually hung out. The top was lying askew, tipped toward the back.

"I guess I didn't put the lid on tight enough," Max said. "I've been really scared. I thought maybe Marmaduke ate him."

"That would have been gross," Tim said.

"It would have been awful!" Max said. He lifted Flamester from around his neck and held him out to Tim. "Want to hold him?" he asked.

Tim shook his head. "No. No, thanks."

Flamester curled himself 'round and 'round Max's hands and wrists. Part of him hung down from Max's arm, flipping back and forth. Emma watched. She knew it was possible for someone to love a snake as much as she loved her ferret. But she didn't really understand how.

"Snakes can't climb walls, can they?" Emma asked. "So maybe Marmaduke's cage should go up on a shelf?"

"Marmaduke's cage?" Auntie Liz said. "What do you mean, *Marmaduke*?"

She was standing in Max's doorway. Her hair was all spiky, her face creased with sleep lines from her pillow. Uncle Max was beside her, his face scrunched up into a frown, his head tilted to one side.

"Marmaduke?" Auntie Liz repeated. "Emma's ferret? He's not here. Is he?"

Emma looked down. *Yup. He is. Right over there. Don't come in. Please.*

Uncle Max wrinkled up his forehead. There was a lot of it because he was kind of bald. "Tim? Emma? Isn't it—like—midnight or something?"

Emma looked at her Mickey Mouse watch. "Almost," she said.

Uncle Max moved farther into the room and plopped down on the bed. He rubbed his eyes and yawned. "I guess there's a reason you two are here?" he said.

"We needed to help find Flamester," Emma said. "But he's found. So we can go home now." She sent a look to Tim, then started for the door.

"That snake's always disappearing," Uncle Max said. "But hold on a minute. What's this about Marmaduke?"

"Nothing!" Emma said. "I mean, we were just talking about how ferrets eat snakes. I mean, some ferrets do. I don't think Marmaduke would, though. That's all I was saying."

Uncle Max opened his eyes. He tilted his head at Emma. "You were, eh?" he said. "But we don't have to worry about that here, do we? I mean, there're no ferrets here. Right?"

"Uh, right!" Emma said.

Just one ferret. Right there. And all Uncle Max had to do was look that way.

Oh, well. She couldn't hide him anymore. He was

right there. It would be a relief, anyway. Emma was tired. Tired of hiding things and tired of feeling guilty.

She took a deep breath. "Um," she said. "Well, actually, I guess there is. I mean, there's one ferret, anyway." And then very fast, she said, "Marmadukeishere."

Emma waited for the explosion. It didn't come. Just silence.

"WehadtofindFlamesterbeforeMarmadukeatehim," she added.

Still silence.

Emma felt something welling up inside her. It was awful. It was terrible.

It was laughter.

She was going to laugh.

Auntie Liz would kill her.

And if Auntie Liz didn't, Uncle Max would.

But Emma couldn't help it. The laughter just kept welling up inside. She caught Tim's eye. He was going to laugh, too!

Emma tried to think of something sad. Her tree. Terrible Mr. Thompson. Woof throwing up in her lap.

It didn't work. The laugh kept bubbling up.

There were footsteps in the hall. A light came on.

Auntie Liz turned toward the footsteps.

And Annie came bursting into the room.

"Emma? Tim?" she said. "Oh, me dears, I was worried. Woof was going crazy. Running back and forth like a wild dog, he was, and you were missing. Your beds were empty and your mum and daddy got up and . . ."

And suddenly, Emma didn't feel at all like laughing anymore.

Chapter Twenty

Emma Tells All

It was morning.

The explosion that Emma had expected the night before hadn't happened, at least, not right away. Mom had insisted that the kids all go to bed and stay there! And when it did come in the morning, it wasn't an explosion so much as a big fat surprise.

The family, all but the little kids and Annie who were hovering around Marmaduke in his cage out on the lawn, had gathered on the porch. Max and Uncle Max and Auntie Liz were there, too.

Emma told the whole story right from the beginning, and she told the truth, too—how she had sneaked Marmaduke into her backpack, and how Woof had thrown up and how Annie had stopped to buy the cage, and everything. And how it was not Annie's fault.

"Well, I don't know about that," Mom said. "Annie might have thought about turning around and taking Marmaduke back home."

Emma shook her head. "She couldn't. She didn't find out till we were a hundred kilometers from home!"

Daddy raised his eyebrows.

"And then," Emma said, "when we got here, I was going to tell right away. I really was. Annie told me I had to. But then I found out about Mr. Thompson cutting down the trees and I knew you'd ground me because of Marmaduke, so I had to hide him until I cut the tape off and saved my tree, but it didn't work anyway, and . . ."

"And it was my fault, too," Max said.

"But I suggested it," Emma said.

"Yes," Daddy said. "Both of you are at fault. But let's forget Marmaduke for a minute and talk about something bigger—the trees. We, that is, Mom, I, and Uncle Max and Auntie Liz, we talked last night after you kids were in bed. We think it's partly our fault about the trees. We set a bad example, I'm afraid, telling you that the Thompsons were terrible people and . . ."

Emma wanted to interject, "impossible people." But she knew better.

"And," Daddy went on, "they're not. They have

a right to do what they want on their property. Mr. Thompson is a very fine man."

Ha! Emma thought.

"But," Daddy went on, "we might have made you think it was okay to try and save the trees because—"

"Because we didn't want the trees to come down, either," Auntie Liz said.

"And," Mom said, "we know that. So we're partly responsible. But that doesn't lessen your responsibility. And I don't like all these secrets. I'm disappointed in all three of you."

"Tim didn't do anything," Emma said.

"Well, I kind of did," Tim said. "I mean, I knew about Marmaduke before last night. And I didn't tell."

"You knew?" Mom said.

Tim nodded.

"When did you find out?" Mom asked.

"At the barbecue," Tim said.

"How?"

"Remember? Auntie Liz said we could go get her glasses," Tim said. "Me and McClain. So we went, and McClain went into Max's room for a toy and saw Marmaduke and—"

"McClain?" Mom said. "McClain knew, too?"

Again, Tim nodded.

125

"So you all knew?" Mom said.

"Well," Emma said, "not the twins."

"And nobody said anything?" Mom said.

Emma and Tim looked at one another. They both shrugged.

There was a long moment of quiet. Mom turned to Daddy. She put both hands to her head. "We're outnumbered," she said softly.

Daddy nodded. "I'm afraid so. Seems like a conspiracy to me."

Mom and Daddy kept on exchanging looks. But suddenly, Emma thought it was okay. She was pretty sure it was okay. Because she could tell that both Mom and Daddy were trying not to laugh.

After a minute, Daddy turned away from Mom and back to Emma and Tim and Max.

"Get out of here," he said, waving his hand. "All of you! Go swimming or something."

Emma jumped to her feet. "Really?" she said. "You mean I'm not grounded?"

Daddy frowned. "Tomorrow," he said. "We'll start grounding you tomorrow."

Emma had a feeling, though, that he didn't mean that at all.

Chapter Twenty-one
Saving Poochie

Emma lay flat on her back on the raft in the sun. Max and Tim lay beside her. Woof, too. They had all swum out to the raft and were sunning themselves, warming up after the cold water. They were talking about grown-ups.

Emma had known for a long time that grown-ups were very, very weird. But now, she was sure of it. Sometimes, when Emma had done a little bad thing, the grown-ups had made a huge deal over it. And other times, like now, when she had done something really, really naughty, they didn't seem so very, very mad.

Emma sat up and looked around her at the lake. For the first time since the family had arrived in Maine, she was happy. Relieved. She didn't have any bad secrets. She so much loved this place, the lake, these trees. Off in the distance, she could see ducks paddling around and at least one loon. Loons were really loony. They made weird calls that sounded as if they were laughing. They could dive down, swim for a long, long way underwater —and then surface far, far away. Emma thought it would be great fun to be able to hold her breath that long. She was a strong swimmer, but she could never do that.

Now, as she sat looking around, she heard the hum of that little motorboat, the one McClain had said sounded like bees.

She sent a look to Tim, to Max. She screwed up her face. Mr. Thompson. Okay, she'd be nice to him. But she didn't have to like him.

His boat puttered up to the foot of their dock, his fat little dog on the seat behind him. He waved to them, then turned and reached for his little dog after tying up the boat. They both clambered up onto the dock.

That's when Woof decided it would be polite to go and say hello.

He leaped off the raft and swam toward Mr. Thompson and Poochie. He scrabbled his way onto the dock, too, his paws clicking on the wood. He shook himself hard, spraying water all over Mr. Thompson.

Emma giggled. Mr. Thompson stepped back. He

lost his balance. He didn't fall into the lake. Rats.

But he did let go of Poochie.

And Poochie went tumbling. Off the dock. Backward into the lake.

He sank immediately. And disappeared. Then just as quickly, he bobbed up, his little paws flailing and splashing.

Emma didn't wait even a second. "Come on!" she shouted. She dove off the raft. Tim did, too. Also Max.

For one instant, everything got quiet. They were all great swimmers. But what about Poochie? It seemed he couldn't swim at all.

On the dock, Mr. Thompson was on his knees, frantically reaching out for Poochie. But the dog had surfaced and then sunk again.

All three kids swam furiously. Emma got there first. She dove down, kicking her legs hard. The lake was clear. She could see Poochie. She grabbed a big handful of fur.

She surfaced. Lifted him above the water. He slid out of her grasp. He sank again.

"I'll get him!" Max yelled. "I can see him."

And then, just like that, Poochie bobbed to the surface. He rested there, almost as if he were floating. For just one moment, it seemed that Poochie had learned to swim, the way Woof had, his little head above the water, his paws waving around. It was crazy.

Then Emma realized—Tim! Tim had dived under the surface. The lake was super-clear, and Emma could see Tim beneath the water, paddling with just one hand. The other hand was under Poochie's little body. Tim's fingers were outspread, pushing Poochie's body upward.

In a moment, Tim and Poochie both shot above the water. But Poochie had flung himself around, and now all Tim had of him was his tail. Still, Tim paddled strongly toward Emma, towing Poochie behind. Emma reached out.

"He's heavy!" Tim yelled. "Don't let go."

"Oh, please, don't let go! Don't!" Mr. Thompson yelled.

Emma reached out and grabbed a handful of fur. Got him right behind his neck! She lifted him above the water. Poochie was slimy, slippery. And so little under all that wet. But he was in Emma's grasp. Alive. Mad, too, from the way he was thrashing around.

"Hand him to me, hand him to me!" Mr. Thompson yelled.

But Emma wasn't about to do that. Even from the water, she could see that Mr. Thompson was shaking like one of his trees. He was sure to drop

Poochie, and they'd have to rescue him all over again.

"Max!" Emma yelled. "Get up on the dock. I'll hand him over. Tim! You get up there and get Woof!"

That's because Woof was prancing around the dock, barking and still trying to be polite and say hello, all the while that Poochie was fighting for his life in the water.

Tim grabbed the edge of the dock and launched himself up. He got hold of Woof by his collar. "Stop it, stop it, Woof!" he cried.

Max hauled himself onto the dock, too. He reached down.

Emma paddled to him, still holding the fat little dog by the back of his neck. Max slid both hands under and around Poochie. He scooped him up onto the dock.

Poochie was safe!

Max handed him over, and Mr. Thompson hugged Poochie like crazy. Emma thought there were even tears in Mr. Thompson's eyes.

Emma climbed onto the dock, too, shaking her streaming wet hair out of her eyes and blinking hard against the sun. She watched Mr. Thompson cooing and crooning over Poochie, and she had a sudden and very weird thought. Maybe it was a good thing that they'd been able to save Mr. Thompson's fat little dog. Maybe it made up—at least a little bit—for all the trouble she had caused him.

Chapter Twenty-two
Home at Last

The wonderful, glorious outdoor summer had drawn to a close. Everybody was tanned and rested. Daddy had grown a funny red beard. The twins had learned more and more words and had learned to swim. Now, if a grown-up were swimming beside them, they could paddle their way all the way to the raft, even though they still had little Floaties on their arms.

McClain had finally managed to catch a chipmunk in her shoebox trap. The chipmunk had scampered out immediately, but it had made McClain very happy, anyway.

Tim had discovered lots of things about the sky and the stars with his new telescope. After helping save Poochie, Tim had even gone into the woods a few times with Max and Emma. It seemed to Emma that Tim had gotten a little of his courage back.

And Max and Emma, after being grounded for only one day, had done absolutely nothing but run around, swim, climb trees, and lie on the dock and watch the stars.

And Annie, who had never seen anything like the woods of Maine, was so enchanted that she had asked Mom and Daddy if her sisters could come and visit next summer. Mom and Daddy had said the sisters could have the house for the entire month of September if they wanted.

Finally, they had arrived back home. Emma couldn't wait to see Marshmallow. She hoped Marshmallow hadn't forgotten her. She was sure Marshmallow hadn't forgotten Marmaduke. They would be so happy to be together again.

But before they all went into the house, Daddy had to take that family picture.

They lined up on the steps, silly and happy, not really posing, just playing around. McClain sat on Lizzie's lap, almost squashing her. Ira leaped into Tim's lap. Ira had stolen Kelley from McClain and was hugging Kelley under his chin, just the way McClain did. Mom and Annie were leaning close, their heads together, arms around one another. And right in the front, Emma sat with Woof. Emma posed just the way Woof did—she sat straight, head up, pretending to be a dog. And holding tightly on to Marmaduke.

When they were all finished, and after they had switched places so Daddy could be in the picture and after Emma had let Tim hold Marmaduke, they started for the house.

Daddy called to Emma. "Wait a minute, honey," he said. "I want to show you something."

"Can't it wait?" Emma said. "I want to call Luisa! I want her to bring over Marshmallow."

"In a minute," Daddy said. "Come on. Come with me."

She frowned. "Daddy!"

"Really," Daddy said. "Come on. It's important. It will only take a minute."

He took her hand. In his other hand, he held something by his side, as if he were hiding it from her. They walked around the house to the back. There was the wide yard, the swings and climbing bars, the basketball hoop, and the long stretch of grass and lawn. The windows of Emma's room looked right down on this grassy part.

Daddy stopped. "So, what do you think?" he said.

"What?" Emma asked.

"Look!" Daddy said.

Emma looked. Something was different. But what? She tilted her head, puzzling it out.

And then she saw it. A tree. There was a tree right below her window. It was ringed with stakes and rubber band–type things to support it. It was tall, reaching up almost to her window. It was slender— a beautiful, tall, slender tree. A tree that had not been there before.

"Daddy?" Emma said. "What is it, Daddy? I mean, I know it's a tree. But where did it come from? I mean . . ."

"It's a special tree," Daddy said. "It's called a flowering pear. It doesn't get pears on it, so I don't know why it's called that. But it does get flowers on it. Lots and lots of white flowers. In the springtime."

"Oh, Daddy!" Emma cried. "Oh, Daddy, did you do this? Did you remember? About Anne? Is that why . . . ?"

Daddy shook his head. "No," he said. "No. I didn't do it."

He handed Emma the thing he'd been hiding.

Emma took it. She looked down. It was a book. No, not just any book. It was her book! It was *Anne of Green Gables*. All worn out and beat up, the very book she had lost that awful day in the tree.

There was a note attached. Emma opened it.

"I read your book," the note said. "I wanted you to have your very own tree outside your very own window. Just as Anne does."

The note was signed: Tommy Thompson.

Emma bit her lip. She looked at Daddy, then she looked away. Tears sprang to her eyes. Not bad tears.

She wanted to say something, but she couldn't. Not out loud, anyway. But she thought it. She thought it really, really hard. *Maybe*, she thought, *maybe Mr. Thompson wasn't really such a bad man after all.*